"You can't push me away."

Jackson lifted her chin with his fingers so she couldn't avoid his gaze. Their faces were only a few inches apart.

"What if I am crazy?" Allie's voice broke. "Crazy like a fox?" The first of the fireworks exploded, showering down a glittering red, white and blue light on the meadow below them. The boom echoed in her chest as another exploded to the "oohs" and "ahhs" of the wedding party. She felt scalding tears burn her throat.

Jackson couldn't bear to see Allie like this. He pulled her to him and, dropping his mouth to hers, kissed her. She leaned into him, letting him draw her even closer as the kiss deepened. Fireworks lit the night, booming in a blaze of glittering light before going dark again.

Desire ignited his blood. He wanted Allie like he'd never wanted anyone or anything before.

WEDDING AT CARDWELL RANCH

New York Times Bestselling Author

B.J. DANIELS

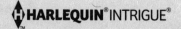

Recycling programs
for this product may
not exist in your area.

This is dedicated to my readers and my
Facebook friends who shared their "gaslighting"
ideas and proved that they think as creepy me.

If you haven't already, come say hello on my
author Facebook page at www.facebook.com/
pages/BJ-Daniels/127936587217837.

Thanks for stopping by Cardwell Ranch!

ISBN-13: 978-0-373-69770-0

WEDDING AT CARDWELL RANCH

Copyright © 2014 by Barbara Heinlein

Printed in U.S.A.

ABOUT THE AUTHOR

New York Times bestselling author B.J. Daniels wrote her first book after a career as an award-winning newspaper journalist and author of thirty-seven published short stories. That first book, *Odd Man Out,* received a four-and-a-half-star review from *RT Book Reviews* and went on to be nominated for Best Intrigue that year. Since then, she has won numerous awards, including a career achievement award for romantic suspense and many nominations and awards for best book.

Daniels lives in Montana with her husband, Parker, and two springer spaniels, Spot and Jem. When she isn't writing, she snowboards, camps, boats and plays tennis. Daniels is a member of Mystery Writers of America, Sisters in Crime, International Thriller Writers, Kiss of Death and Romance Writers of America.

To contact her, write to B.J. Daniels, P.O. Box 1173, Malta, MT 59538, or email her at bjdaniels@mtintouch.net. Check out her website, www.bjdaniels.com.

Books by B.J. Daniels

HARLEQUIN INTRIGUE

CAST OF CHARACTERS

Jackson Cardwell—The Texas cowboy only came to Montana with his son Ford to attend his brother Tag's wedding, not to get involved with the wedding planner.

Allie Knight Taylor—The widowed wedding planner thought she was losing her mind—until she met the Texas cowboy and lost her heart.

Natalie Taylor—The five-year-old was worried about her mother, Allie. Did she have good reason to worry?

Belinda Andrews—The wedding photographer was Allie's best friend. Or was she?

Megan Fairchild—Allie's half sister only wanted what was best for her sister and niece, right?

Nick Taylor—While legally dead, he wasn't forgotten, since he was still haunting his wife, Allie.

Drew Taylor—He wanted the woman his brother Nick had married. But was he willing to kill to have Allie?

Mildred Taylor—Everyone was afraid of the matriarch of the family and would do anything she asked. But how far would she go?

Sarah Taylor—To her mother's disgust, she found solace in food and liked her life exactly as it was.

Chapter One

Allison Taylor brushed back a lock of her hair and willed herself not to scream.

"Is something wrong?" her brother-in-law asked from the kitchen doorway, startling her and making her jump.

She dropped the heavy covered pot she'd taken from the pantry a little too hard onto the counter. The lid shifted, but not enough that she could see inside.

"Didn't mean to scare you," Drew Taylor said with a laugh as he lounged against the kitchen door frame. "I was cravin' some of your famous chili, but I think maybe we should go out."

"I just need a minute. If you could see to Natalie…"

"She's still asleep. I just checked." Drew studied her for a long moment. Like his brother, he had russet-brown hair and dark brown eyes and classic good looks. His mother had assured both of her sons that they were wonderful. Fortunately Drew had taken it with a grain of salt—unlike his brother Nick.

"Are you okay, Allie? I've been so worried about you since Nick…"

"I'm fine." She didn't want to talk about her presumed-dead husband. She really just wanted her brother-in-law to go into the other room and leave her alone for a moment.

Drew had been a godsend. She didn't know what she would have done without him, she thought as she pulled a band from her jeans pocket and secured her long, blond hair in a single tail at the back of her head.

When she'd mentioned how nice his brother was to Nick shortly after they married, he'd scoffed.

"Just be glad he likes you. He's about the only one in my family," he had added with a laugh.

"Why don't you let me help you with that," Drew said now as he took a step toward her. He frowned as his gaze went to the pot and the pile of ingredients she'd already stacked up on the counter. The chili pot was the last thing she'd brought into the kitchen from the porch of the small cabin. "You kept the pot?"

So his mother had told him about the incident.

He must think I'm losing my mind just like his mother and sister do.

The worst part was she feared they were right.

Allie looked down at the heavy cast-iron pot with its equally heavy cast-iron lid. Her hand trembled as she reached for the handle. The memory of the last time she'd lifted that lid—and what she'd found inside—sent a shudder through her.

The covered cast-iron casserole pot, enameled white inside and the color of fresh blood on the outside, had been a wedding present from her in-laws.

"She does know how to cook, doesn't she?" her mother-in-law, Mildred, had asked all those years ago as if Allie hadn't been standing there. Mildred was a twig-thin woman who took pride in these things: her petite, slim, fifty-eight-year-old body, her sons and her standing in the community. Her daughter, Sarah, was just the opposite of her mother, overweight and dumpy by comparison. And Mildred was always making that comparison to anyone who would listen, including Sarah.

Mildred was on her fourth husband and lived in one of

the more modest mansions at Big Sky. Of her two sons, Nick had been the baby—and clearly her favorite.

Nick had laughed that day when his mother had asked if his new wife could cook. "She makes pretty good chili, I'll give her that," he told Mildred. "But that's not why I married her." He'd given Allie a side hug, grinning like a fool and making her blush to the roots of her hair.

Nick had liked to say he had the prettiest wife in town. "Just make sure you stay that way," he'd always add. "You start looking like my sister and you can pack your bags."

The red, cast-iron, covered pot she was now reaching for had become her chili pot.

"Allie, I thought you'd thrown that pot away!" Drew reached to stop her, knocking the lid off in the effort. It clattered to the counter.

Allie lunged back, her arm going up protectively to shield her face. But this time the pot was empty. No half-dead squirrel inside it.

"I'm throwing this pot in the trash," Drew announced. "If just the sight of it upsets you—"

"No, your mother will have a fit."

"Let her." He swept pot and lid off the counter and carried it out to the garbage can.

When he came back into the room, he looked at her and shook his head. "Allie, you've got to pull it together. Maybe you should go back to the doctor and see if there is something else he can give you. You're strung like a piano wire."

She shook her head. "I don't need a doctor." She just needed for whatever was happening to her to stop.

His gaze moved past her, his expression going from a concerned frown to a smile. "Hey, girl," he said as his five-year-old niece came into the kitchen. He stepped past Allie to swing Nat into his arms. "I came over to check on the two of you. Mama was going to cook us some dinner but I think we should go out to eat. What do you say?"

Allie started to argue that she couldn't let Drew do any more for them and she sure couldn't afford to go out to eat, but stopped as her daughter said, "Are you sick, Mama?" Her precious daughter looked to her with concern. Allie saw the worry in Nat's angelic face. She'd seen it too much lately. It was bad enough that Natalie had recently lost her father. Now more than ever she needed her mother to be sane.

"I'm fine, sweetie. It's too hot for chili, anyway. So let's go out, why not?" Allie said, relieved and thankful for Drew. Not just for coming by to check on them, but for throwing out the pot. She hadn't because her mother-in-law was upset enough and the Taylors were the only family she had, especially now.

"Just let me freshen up and change," she said as Drew took Nat to look for her shoes.

In the bathroom, Allie locked the door, turned on the shower and stripped off her clothes. She was still sweating from fear, her heart beating hard against her chest.

"You found a what in the chili pot?" her mother-in-law had asked in disbelief when Allie had called her—a huge mistake in retrospect. But at the time, she'd hoped her mother-in-law would understand why she couldn't keep the pot. Why she didn't want it in her house.

"I found a squirrel in that cast-iron pot you gave me. When I picked up the lid—"

"No way would a squirrel get into your cabin, let alone climb under a heavy lid like that. Why would it? You must have imagined it. Are you still on those drugs the doctor gave you after my Nicky died?"

Allie's husband had always been "my Nicky" to his mother while Mildred had insisted Allie call *her* "Mother Taylor."

"No, Mother Taylor, I told you." Allie's own mother had died when she was nineteen. Her father had moved, remarried and started a new family. They'd lost touch. "I quit taking the pills a long time ago."

"I think it's those pills," Mildred had said as if Allie hadn't spoken. "You said they had you seeing things that weren't there."

"The squirrel *was* there. I had to take it out back and—"

"If I were you, I'd talk to your doctor. Why do you need the pills, anyway? It isn't like you're still grieving over my Nicky. Charlotte Reynolds told me she saw you having lunch the other day, you and Natalie, and you were *laughing*."

Allie had closed her eyes, remembering the lunch in question. "I am trying to make things more normal for Nat."

"Well, it looks bad, you having a good time while your poor husband is barely cold in his grave."

She wanted to mention that Nick wasn't in his grave, but knew better than to bring that up. "It's been eight months."

"Like you have to tell me that!" Mildred sniffed and blew her nose. She'd cried constantly over the death of her favorite son and couldn't understand why Allie wasn't still doing the same.

"We all grieve in our own way and I have a young daughter to raise," Allie had said more times than she wanted to recall.

The phone call had ended with Mildred crying and talking about what a wonderful man her Nicky had been. A lie at best. He'd been a lousy husband and an even worse father, but now that he was dead, he would always be the wonderful man Mildred remembered.

After that, she'd learned her lesson. She kept the other crazy things that had been happening to herself. If Mildred knew, she would have her in a straitjacket. And little Nat…? She couldn't bear to think about Mildred having anything to do with raising her daughter.

"So," Drew said as she and Nat sat across from him in a

booth at a local café later that evening. "Did I hear you've gone back to work?"

It was impossible to keep anything a secret in this canyon, Allie thought. She had hoped to keep it from the Taylor family as long as possible.

"Dana Savage called me about doing a Western wedding up at her ranch for her cousin Tag and his soon-to-be wife, Lily." She didn't mention that she'd accepted the job several months ago. Or how badly she needed the money. With the investigation into Nick's presumed death still unresolved, the insurance company was holding off paying her. Not that it would last long if she didn't get back to work.

Her mother-in-law kept mentioning "that big insurance check my Nicky left you," but the insurance money would barely cover a couple years of Natalie's college, if that. And Allie hoped to invest it for that very use.

"I've been doing some work at Cardwell Ranch. Nice people to work for. But are you sure you're up to it?" Drew asked quietly, real concern in his tone. "Mother mentioned that she was worried about you. She said you were still taking the pills and they were making you see things?"

Of course Mildred told Drew and his sister, Sarah, everything. Allie tried not to show her irritation. She had no appetite, but she attempted to eat what she could. She didn't want Drew mentioning to his mother, even accidentally, that she wasn't eating much. Mildred would make it into her not taking care of herself.

"I'm fine. I'm *not* taking the pills. I told your mother—"

He held up his hand. "You don't have to tell me about my mother. She hears only what she wants to hear. I'm on your side. I think going back to work might be the best thing for you. So what do you plan to do with Natalie? I don't have to tell you what Mother is going to say."

"Nat's going with me," Allie said emphatically. "Dana

has children she can play with. As a matter of fact, Dana is going to teach Nat to ride a horse."

Natalie grinned and clapped her small hands excitedly. She was the spitting image of Allie at that age: straight, pale blond hair cut in a bob, green eyes with a pert little nose and deep dimples. Allie got the blond hair from her Scandinavian mother and the green eyes from her Irish father.

There was no sign of the Taylor family in her daughter, something that had caused a lot of speculation from not only Nick, but his mother.

Nat quickly told her uncle that it would be a very gentle horse and Dana's kids Hank and Mary were riding before they were even her age. "The twins are too young to ride yet," she announced.

"Dana wouldn't let Nat do it if she thought it wasn't all right," Allie added.

"I'm sure it will be fine," Drew said, but she could tell that he already knew what her mother-in-law was going to have to say about it. "Cardwell Ranch is where the wedding is going to be, I take it?"

"The wedding will be in a meadow on the ranch with the reception and a lot of other events in the large, old barn."

"You know that we've been invited," Drew said almost in warning.

The canyon was its own little community, with many of the older families—like Dana's—that dated back to the eighteen hundreds before there was even a paved road through it. Mildred Taylor must be delighted to be invited to a wedding of a family that was like old canyon royalty. Mother Taylor might resent the Cardwell clan, say things behind their back, but she would never outright defy them since everyone loved Dana Cardwell Savage and had held great respect for her mother, Mary Justice.

"How are things with you?" Allie asked.

"Everything's fine." He smiled but she'd seen the lines

around his eyes and had heard that his construction company was struggling without Nick.

He'd been so generous with her and Natalie that she feared he was giving away money he didn't have.

She was just thankful when the meal was over and Drew dropped her and Nat off at the small cabin in the Gallatin Canyon where she'd lived with Nick until his disappearance. *The canyon* as it was known, ran from the mouth just south of Gallatin Gateway almost to West Yellowstone, fifty miles of winding road that trailed the river in a deep cut through the mountains.

The drive along the Gallatin River was breathtaking, a winding strip of highway that followed the blue-ribbon trout stream up over the Continental Divide. In the summer as it was now, the Gallatin ran crystal clear over tinted green boulders. Pine trees grew dark and thick along its edge and against the steep mountains. Aspens, their leaves bright green, grew among the pines.

Sheer rock cliffs overlooked the highway and river, with small areas of open land. The canyon had been mostly cattle and dude ranches, a few summer cabins and homes—that was until Big Sky resort and the small town that followed developed at the foot of Lone Mountain.

Luxury houses had sprouted up all around the resort, with Mother Taylor's being one of them. Fortunately, some of the original cabins still remained and the majority of the canyon was National Forest so it would always remain undeveloped.

Allie's was one of the older cabins. Because it was small and not in great shape, Nick had gotten a good deal on it. Being in construction, he'd promised to enlarge it and fix all the things wrong with it. That hadn't happened.

After Drew left, Allie didn't hurry inside the cabin. It was a nice summer night, the stars overhead glittering brightly and a cool breeze coming up from the river.

She had begun to hate the cabin—and her fear of what might be waiting for her inside it. Nick had been such a force of nature to deal with that his presence seemed to have soaked into the walls. Sometimes she swore she could hear his voice. Often she found items of his clothing lying around the house as if he was still there—even though she'd boxed up his things and taken them to the local charity shop months ago.

Just the thought of what might be waiting for her inside the cabin this time made her shudder as she opened the door and stepped in, Nat at her side.

She hadn't heard Nick's voice since she'd quit taking the drugs. Until last night. When she'd come into the living room, half-asleep, she'd found his favorite shirt lying on the floor by the couch. She'd actually thought she smelled his aftershave even though she'd thrown the bottle away.

The cabin looked just as she'd left it. Letting out a sigh of relief, she put Nat to bed and tried to convince herself she hadn't heard Nick's voice last night. Even the shirt that she'd remembered picking up and thinking it felt warm and smelled of Nick before she'd dropped it over the back of the couch was gone this morning, proving the whole incident had been nothing but a bad dream.

"Good night, sweetheart," she said and kissed her daughter's forehead.

"Night," Nat said sleepily and closed her eyes.

Allie felt as if her heart was going to burst when she looked at her precious daughter. She couldn't let Mildred get her hands on Nat. But if the woman thought for a moment that Allie was incapable of raising her daughter...

She quickly turned out the light and tiptoed out of the room. For a moment, she stood in the small living area. Nick's shirt wasn't over the back of the couch so that was a relief.

So many times she had stood here and wished her life

could be different. Nick had been so sweet while they were dating. She'd really thought she'd met her Prince Charming—until after the wedding and she met the real Nick Taylor.

She sighed, remembering her decision soon after the wedding to leave him and have the marriage annulled, but then she'd realized she was pregnant. Had she really been so naive as to think a baby would change Nick into the man she'd thought she'd married?

Shaking her head now, she looked around the cabin, remembering all the ideas she had to fix the place up and make it a home. Nick had hated them all and they had ended up doing nothing to the cabin.

Well, she could do what she wanted now, couldn't she? But she knew, even if she had the money, she didn't have the heart for it. She would never be able to exorcize Nick's ghost from this house. What she really wanted was to sell the cabin and move. She promised herself she would—once everything with Nick's death was settled.

Stepping into her bedroom, she was startled to see a pile of her clothes on her bed. Had she taken them out of the closet earlier when she'd changed to go to dinner? Her heart began to pound. She'd been upset earlier but she wouldn't have just thrown her clothes on the bed like that.

Then how had they gotten there? She'd locked the cabin when she'd left.

Panicked, she raced through the house to see if anything was missing or if any of the doors or windows had been broken into. Everything was just as she'd left it—except for the clothes on her bed.

Reluctantly, she walked back into her bedroom half-afraid the clothes wouldn't still be on the bed. Another hallucination?

The clothes were there. Unfortunately, that didn't come as a complete relief. Tonight at dinner, she'd worn capris, a blouse and sandals since it was June in Montana. Why would she have pulled out what appeared to be almost everything she owned from the closet? No, she realized, not *everything*. These were only the clothes that Nick had bought her.

Tears blurred her eyes as she started to pick up one of the dresses. Like the others, she hated this dress because it reminded her of the times he'd made her wear it and how the night had ended. It was very low cut in the front. She'd felt cheap in it and told him so but he'd only laughed.

"When you've got it, flaunt it," he'd said. "That's what I say."

Why hadn't she gotten rid of these clothes? For the same reason she hadn't thrown out the chili pot after the squirrel incident. She hadn't wanted to upset her mother-in-law. Placating Mother Taylor had begun right after Allie had married her son. It was just so much easier than arguing with the woman.

"Nick said you don't like the dresses he buys you," Mildred had said disapprovingly one day when she'd stopped by the cabin and asked Allie why she wasn't wearing the new dress. "There is nothing wrong with looking nice for your husband."

"The dresses he buys me are just more revealing than I feel comfortable with."

Her mother-in-law had mugged a face. "You'd better loosen up and give my son what he wants or he'll find someone who will."

Now as she reached for the dress on the top of the pile, she told herself she would throw them out, Mother Taylor be damned.

But the moment she touched the dress, she let out a cry of surprise and panic. The fabric had jagged cuts down the front. She stared in horror as she saw other deep, angry-looking slices in the fabric. *Who had done this?*

Her heart in her throat, she picked up another of the
dresses Nick had made her wear. Her sewing scissors clattered to the bedroom floor. She stared down at the scissors
in horror, then at the pile of destroyed clothing. All of the
dresses Nick had bought her had been ruined.

Allie shook her head as she dropped the dress in her
hand and took a step back from the bed. Banging into the
closed closet doors, she fought to breathe, her heart ham-
mering in her chest. *Who did this?* Who *would* do this? She
remembered her brother-in-law calling from out in the hall
earlier, asking what was taking her so long before they'd
gone to dinner. But that was because she'd taken a shower
to get the smell of her own fear off her. It wasn't because
she was in here cutting up the clothes her dead husband
had made her wear.

Tears welled in her eyes, making the room blur. She
shoved that bitter thought away and wiped at her tears. She
wouldn't have done this. She *couldn't* have.

Suddenly, she turned and stared at the closed closet door
with mounting fear. Slowly, she reached for the knob, her
hand trembling. As the closet door came open, she froze.
Her eyes widened in new alarm.

A half dozen new outfits hung in the otherwise nearly
empty closet, the price tags still on them. As if sleepwalk-
ing, Allie reached for one of the tags and stared in shock at
the price. Hurriedly, she checked the others. She couldn't
afford any of them. So where had they come from?

Not only that, the clothes were what she would call "classic," the type of clothes she'd worn when she'd met Nick.
The kind of clothes she'd pleaded with him to let her wear.

"I want other men to look at you and wish they were me,"
Nick had said, getting angry.

But when she and Nick went out and she wore the clothes
and other men did look, Nick had blamed her.

"You must have given him the eye," Nick would say as

they argued on the way home. "Probably flipped your hair like an invitation. Who knows what you do while I'm at work all day."

"I take care of your daughter and your house."

Nick hadn't let her work after they'd gotten married, even though he knew how much she loved her wedding planning business. "Women who work get too uppity. They think they don't need a man. No wife of mine is going to work."

Allie had only the clothes he bought her. She'd purchased little since his death because the money had been so tight. Nick had wanted to know about every cent she'd spent, so she hadn't been able to save any money, either. Nick paid the bills and gave her a grocery allowance. He said he'd buy her whatever she needed.

Now she stared at the beautiful clothes hanging in her closet. Beautiful blouses and tops. Amazing skirts and pants and dresses. Clothes Nick would have taken out in the yard and burned. But Nick was gone.

Or was he? He still hadn't been declared legally dead. That thought scared her more than she wanted to admit. What if he suddenly turned up at her door one night?

Was that what was making her crazy? Maybe she *had* done this. She had yearned for clothing like this and hated the clothes Nick had bought her, so had she subconsciously…

Allie stumbled away from the closet, bumped into the corner of the bed and sat down hard on the floor next to it. Her hand shook as she covered her mouth to keep from screaming. Had she shoplifted these clothes? She couldn't have purchased them. Just as she couldn't have cut up the dresses and not remembered. There had to be another explanation. Someone was playing a horrible trick on her.

But even as she pondered it, more rational thoughts came on its heels. Did she really believe that someone had come into the cabin and done this? Who in their right mind would believe that?

Pushing herself up, she crawled over to where she'd dropped her purse as she tried to remember even the last time she'd written a check. Her checkbook wasn't in her purse. She frowned and realized she must have left it in the desk when she'd paid bills.

Getting up she walked on wobbly legs to the desk in the corner, opened the drawer and took out her checkbook. Her fingers shook with such a tremor that she could barely read what was written in it.

But there it was. A check for more than eight hundred dollars! The handwriting was scrawled, but she knew it had to be hers. She saw the date of the check. *Yesterday?*

She had dropped Nat off for a playdate and then gone into Bozeman… Could she account for the entire afternoon? Her heart pounded as she tried to remember everything she'd done and when she might have bought these clothes. She'd been wandering around in a daze since Nick's death. She couldn't account for every minute of yesterday, but what did that matter? The proof was staring her in the face.

Allie shoved the checkbook into the drawer and tried to pull herself together. She had to think about her daughter.

"You're fine," she whispered to herself. "Once you get back to work…" She couldn't have been more thankful that she had the Cardwell Ranch wedding. More than the money, she needed to do what she loved—planning weddings—and get her mind off everything else.

Once she was out of this house she'd shared with Nick… Yes, then she would be fine. She wouldn't be so…forgetful. What woman wouldn't feel she was losing her mind, considering what she'd been going through?

Chapter Two

"Who's that singing?" five-year-old Ford Cardwell asked as he and his father followed the sound.

Jackson Cardwell had parked the rental SUV down by his cousin Dana's ranch house when they'd arrived, but finding no one at home, they'd headed up the hill toward the barn and the van parked in front of it.

"I have no idea, son," Jackson said, but couldn't help smiling. The voice was young and sweet, the song beautiful. "It sounds like an angel."

"It *is* an angel," Ford cried and pointed past the barn to the corrals.

The girl was about his son's age, but while Ford had taken after the Cardwell side of the family with his dark hair and eyes, this child had pale blond hair and huge green eyes.

When she saw them, she smiled, exposing two deep dimples. Both children were adorable, but this little girl was hands down more angelic-looking and—Jackson would bet—*acting* than Ford.

She wore cowboy boots with a pale green-and-white-polka-dotted, one-piece, short jumpsuit that brought out the emerald-green of her eyes. Jackson saw that the girl was singing to several horses that had come up to the edge of the corral fence.

The girl finished the last of the lyrics before she seemed

to notice them and came running over. "If you're looking for my mother, she's in the barn working."

Next to him, Jackson saw that his son had apparently been struck dumb.

"I'm Nat," the girl announced. "My name is really Natalie, though." She shifted her gaze to the mute Ford. "Everyone calls me Nat, so you can if you want to."

"This is my son, Ford."

Nat eyed Ford for a moment before she stepped forward and took his hand. "Come on, Ford. You'll probably want to see the rest of the animals. There are chickens and rabbits and several mules along with all the horses. Don't worry," she added before Jackson could voice his concern. "We won't get too close. We'll just pet them through the corral fence and feed the horses apples. It's okay. Mrs. Savage showed me how."

"Don't go far," Jackson said as the precocious Nat led his son toward several low-slung buildings. The girl was busy talking as they left. Ford, as far as Jackson could tell, hadn't uttered a word yet.

As he turned back toward the barn, he saw the logo on the side of the van: Weddings by Allie Knight. The logo looked old as did the van.

The girl had said her mother was working in the barn. That must be where the wedding was going to be held. His brother Tag had mentioned something about his wedding to Lily McCabe being very *Western*.

"You mean like Texas meets Montana?" Jackson had joked.

"Something like that. Don't worry. You'll feel right at home."

His brother's wedding wasn't what had him worried. After talking to Tag for a few moments on the phone, he'd known his brother had fallen head over heels for Lily. He was happy for him.

No, what worried Jackson was nailing down the last of the plans before the wedding for the opening of a Texas Boys Barbecue joint in Big Sky, Montana. He had hoped that all of the brothers would be here by now. Laramie and Austin hadn't even flown up to see the space Tag had found, let alone signed off on the deal.

From the time the five brothers had opened their first restaurant in an old house in Houston, they'd sworn they would never venture outside of Texas with their barbecue. Even as their business had grown and they'd opened more restaurants and finally started their own franchise, they had stayed in the state where they'd been raised.

Jackson understood why Tag wanted to open one here. But he feared it had nothing to do with business and everything to do with love and not wanting to leave Montana, where they had all been born.

Before the wedding had seemed the perfect time for all of them to get together and finalize the deal. Hayes had come here last month to see if the restaurant was even feasible. Unfortunately, Hayes had gotten sidetracked, so now it was up to the rest of them to make sure Tag was doing the best thing for the business—and before the wedding, which was only four days away.

He hoped all his brothers arrived soon so they could get this over with. They led such busy lives in Texas that they hardly ever saw each other. Tag had said on the phone he was anxious to show him the building he'd found for the new restaurant. Tag and Hayes had already made arrangements to buy the building without the final okay from the other brothers, something else that made Jackson nervous.

Jackson didn't want this move to cause problems among the five of them. So his mind was miles away as he started to step into the dim darkness inside the barn.

The cool air inside was suddenly filled with a terrified scream. An instant later, a black cat streaked past him and out the barn door.

JACKSON RACED INTO the barn not sure what he was going to find. What he found was a blond-haired woman who shared a striking resemblance to the little girl who'd been singing outside by the corrals.

While Nat had been angelic, this woman was as beautiful as any he'd ever seen. Her long, straight, blond hair was the color of sunshine. It rippled down her slim back. Her eyes, a tantalizing emerald-green, were huge with fear in a face that could stop traffic.

She stood against the barn wall, a box of wedding decorations open at her feet. Her eyes widened in even more alarm when she saw him. She threw a hand over her mouth, cutting off the scream.

"Are you all right?" he asked. She didn't appear to be hurt, just scared. No, not scared, *terrified.* Had she seen a mouse? Or maybe something larger? In Texas it might have been an armadillo. He wasn't sure what kind of critters they had this far north, but something had definitely set her off.

"It was nothing," she said, removing her hand from her mouth. Some of the color slowly returned to her face but he could see that she was still trembling.

"It was *something,*" he assured her.

She shook her head and ventured a look at the large box of decorations at her feet. The lid had been thrown to the side, some of the decorations spilling onto the floor.

He laughed. "Let me guess. That black cat I just saw hightailing it out of here… I'm betting he came out of that box."

Her eyes widened further. *"You saw it?"*

"Raced right past me." He laughed. "You didn't think you imagined it, did you?"

"It happened so fast. I couldn't be sure."

"Must have given you quite a fright."

She let out a nervous laugh and tried to smile, exposing deep dimples. He understood now why his son had gone mute. He felt the same way looking at Natalie's mother. There was an innocence about her, a vulnerability that would make a man feel protective.

Just the thought made him balk. He'd fallen once and wasn't about to get lured into that trap again. Not that there was any chance of that happening. In a few days he would be on a plane back to Texas with his son.

"You know cats," he said, just being polite. "They'll climb into just about anything. They're attracted by pretty things." Just like some cowboys. Not him, though.

"Yes," she said, but didn't sound convinced as she stepped away from the box. She didn't look all that steady on her feet. He started to reach out to her, but stopped himself as she found her footing.

He couldn't help noticing that her eyes were a darker shade of green than her daughter's. "Just a cat. A black one at that," he said, wondering why he felt the need to fill the silence. "You aren't superstitious, are you?"

She shook her head and those emerald eyes brightened. That with the color returning to her cheeks made her even more striking.

This was how he'd fallen for Ford's mother—a pretty face and what had seemed like a sweet disposition in a woman who'd needed him—and look how that had turned out. No, it took more than a pretty face to turn his head after the beating he'd taken from the last one.

"You must be one of Tag's brothers," she said as she wiped her palms on her jeans before extending a hand. Along with jeans, she wore a checked navy shirt, the sleeves rolled up, and cowboy boots. "I'm Allie Taylor, the wedding planner."

Jackson quickly removed his hat, wondering where he'd

left his manners. His mother had raised him better than this. But even as he started to shake her hand, he felt himself hesitate as if he were afraid to touch her.

Ridiculous, he thought as he grasped her small, ice-cold hand in his larger, much warmer one. "Jackson Cardwell. I saw your van outside. But I thought the name on the side—"

"Taylor is my married name." When his gaze went to her empty ring finger, she quickly added, "I'm a widow." She pulled back her hand to rub the spot where her wedding band had resided not that long ago. There was a thin, white line indicating that she hadn't been widowed long. Or she hadn't taken the band off until recently.

"I believe I met your daughter as my son and I were coming in. Natalie?"

"Yes, my baby girl." Her dimpled smile told him everything he needed to know about her relationship with her daughter. He knew that smile and suspected he had one much like it when he talked about Ford.

He felt himself relax a little. There was nothing dangerous about this woman. She was a single parent, just like him. Only she'd lost her husband and he wished he could get rid of his ex indefinitely.

"Your daughter took my son to see the horses. I should probably check on him."

"Don't worry. Nat has a healthy respect for the horses and knows the rules. Also Warren Fitzpatrick, their hired man, is never far away. He's Dana's semi-retired ranch manager. She says he's a fixture around here and loves the kids. That seems to be his job now, to make sure the kids are safe. Not that there aren't others on the ranch watching out for them, as well. Sorry, I talk too much when I'm…nervous." She took a deep breath and let it out slowly. "I want this wedding to be perfect."

He could tell she was still shaken by the black cat episode. "My brother Tag mentioned that Dana and the kids had almost been killed by some crazy woman. It's good she has someone she trusts keeping an eye on the children, even with everyone else on the ranch watching out for them. Don't worry," he said, looking around the barn. "I'm sure the wedding will be perfect."

The barn was huge and yet this felt almost too intimate standing here talking to her. "I was just about to get Ford and go down to the house. Dana told me she was baking a huge batch of chocolate chip cookies and to help ourselves. I believe she said there would also be homemade lemonade when we got here."

Allie smiled and he realized she'd thought it was an invitation. "I really need to get these decorations—"

"Sorry. I'm keeping you from your work." He took a step back. "Those decorations aren't going to put themselves up."

She looked as if she wasn't so sure of that. The cat had definitely put a scare into her, he thought. She didn't seem sure of anything right now. Allie looked again at the box of decorations, no doubt imagining the cat flying out of it at her.

Glancing at her watch, she said, "Oh, I didn't realize it was so late. Nat and I are meeting a friend for lunch. We need to get going."

Jackson was suddenly aware that he'd been holding his hat since shaking Allie's hand. He quickly put it back on as they walked out of the barn door into the bright sunshine. "My son is quite taken with your daughter," he said, again feeling an unusual need to fill the silence.

"How old is he?"

"Ford's five."

"Same age as Nat."

As they emerged into the beautiful late-June day, Jackson saw the two children and waved. As they came running, Nat was chattering away and Ford was hanging on her every word.

"They do seem to have hit it off." Allie sounded surprised and pleased. "Nat's had a hard time lately. I'm glad to see her making a new friend."

Jackson could see that Allie Taylor had been having a hard time, as well. He realized she must have loved her husband very much. He knew he should say something, but for the life of him he couldn't think of what. He couldn't even imagine a happy marriage. As a vehicle came roaring up the road, they both turned, the moment lost.

"Hey, bro," Tanner "Tag" Cardwell called from the rolled down window of his pickup as he swung into the ranch yard. "I see you made it," he said, getting out to come over and shake his brother's hand before he pulled Jackson into a hug. Tag glanced over at Ford and Natalie and added with a laugh, "Like father like son. If there's a pretty female around, you two will find them."

Jackson shook his head. That had been true when he'd met Ford's mother. But since the divorce and the custody battle, he'd been too busy single-handedly raising his son to even think about women. That's why red flags had gone up when he'd met Allie. There was something about her that had pulled at him, something more than her obvious beauty.

"Dana's right behind me with the kids," Tag said. "Why don't I show you and Ford to your cabin, then you can meet everyone." He pointed up in the pines that covered the mountainside. "Let's grab your bags. It's just a short walk."

Jackson turned to say goodbye to Allie, but she and her daughter had already headed for the old van.

"COME ON, NAT, we're meeting Belinda for lunch," Allie said as the Cardwell men headed for the cabins on the mountain behind the barn. Working here had been a godsend. Nat was having a wonderful time. She loved Dana's children. Hank was a year older than Nat, with Mary being the same age. Dana's twin boys, Angus and Brick, were just over a year and her sister Stacy's daughter, Ella, was a year and a half. Dana had her hands full but Stacy helped out with the younger ones. All of them loved the animals, especially the horses.

True to her word, Dana had made sure Nat had begun her horseback riding lessons. Nat was a natural, Dana had said, and Allie could see it was true.

Their few days here so far had been perfect.

Until the cat, there hadn't been any other incidents.

Her friend Belinda Andrews was waiting for them at a little Mexican food place near Meadow Village at Big Sky. While other friends had gone by the wayside since she'd married Nick six years ago, Belinda hadn't let Nick run her off. Allie suspected that, like her, she didn't have a lot of friends and Nick, while he'd made it clear he didn't like Belinda, had grudgingly put up with her the times they'd crossed paths.

"I hope we didn't keep you waiting," Allie said as she and Nat met Belinda on the patio. "You didn't have any trouble getting off work for the wedding shoot?" Belinda worked for a local photographer, but freelanced weddings. It was how they'd met back when Allie had her own wedding planning business.

Belinda grinned. "All set for the Tag Cardwell and Lily McCabe wedding. I took Dana up on her offer. I'm moving into one of the guest cabins later today!"

Allie wasn't all that surprised. Dana had offered her a cabin, as well, while she was preparing everything for the wedding. But since she lived just down the highway a few miles, Allie thought it best to remain at home for Nat's sake. Her daughter had had enough changes in her life recently.

"You really are excited about this," Allie said, noticing how nice Belinda looked. Her friend was dressed in a crop top and cut-off jeans, her skin tanned. Her dark hair was piled haphazardly up on her head, silver dangly earrings tinkled from her earlobes and, while she looked makeup free, Allie could tell she wasn't.

Belinda looked enchanting, a trick Allie wished she could pull off, she thought. On the way here, she'd pulled her hair up in a ponytail and even though she'd showered this morning, she'd forgone makeup. Nick was always suspicious when she wore it when he wasn't around so she'd gotten out of the habit.

Inside the café, Nat asked if she could play in the nearby area for kids and Allie said she could as long as she didn't argue about coming back to eat when her meal came.

"You look…pale," Belinda said, studying her after they were seated outside on the patio under an umbrella so they could see Nat. "You haven't had anymore of those…incidents, have you?"

Allie almost laughed at that. "I just need to get more sun," she said and picked up her menu to hide behind.

"I know you too well," Belinda said, dragging down the menu so she could look into her eyes. "What's happened *now?*"

"A black cat jumped out of one of my decoration boxes and scared me just before I came over here. And guess what? Someone else saw it." *So there,* she wanted to say, *I don't need my head examined.*

Belinda nodded, studying her. "A *black* cat?"

"Yes, a *black* cat and I didn't imagine it. One of the Cardwell brothers saw it, as well." She couldn't even voice how much of a relief that had been.

"That's all that's happened?"

"That's it." She had to look down at the menu to pull off the lie and was just glad when Belinda didn't question her further. She hadn't told *anyone* about the shredded dresses from her closet or the new clothes she'd taken back. The sales associate hadn't remembered her, but said the afternoon when the clothing was purchased had been a busy one. None of the other sales associates remembered her, but agreed they'd been too busy to say for sure. She'd ended up keeping two of the outfits to wear while working the rehearsal dinner and the wedding.

"I already moved some of my things into the cabin," Belinda said.

Allie couldn't help being surprised. "Already? Why didn't you stop by the barn and say hello?" Allie had suggested Belinda as the wedding photographer and felt responsible and anxious since this was her first wedding in five years.

"You were busy," her friend said. "We can't keep each other from our jobs, right?"

"Right." She loved that Belinda understood that. In truth, Allie had been hesitant to suggest her friend. She didn't want to have to worry about Belinda, not with everything else that she had going on in her life right now. While her friend was a great photographer, sometimes she got sidetracked if a handsome man was around. But when she'd broached the subject with the bride-to-be, Lily had been delighted that it was one other thing she didn't have to worry about.

Dana had been kind enough to offer Belinda a cabin on the ranch for the five-day affair. "It will make it easier for you to get great shots if you're staying up here and experiencing all the wedding festivities," Dana had said. "And any friend of Allie's is a friend of ours."

She and Belinda had been friends since grade school. Lately they hadn't been as close, probably Allie's fault. Belinda was in between men right now, and much wilder, freer and more outspoken than Allie had ever been. But Belinda didn't have a five-year-old daughter, either.

"You have no idea what this means to me," Belinda said now. "I've been dying to photograph a Western wedding for my portfolio."

"Your portfolio?"

Belinda looked embarrassed as if she'd let the cat out of the bag, so to speak. "I'm thinking about opening my own studio."

"That's great." Allie was happy for her friend, although she'd wondered if Belinda had come into some money because it wouldn't be cheap and as far as she knew Belinda lived from paycheck to paycheck like everyone else she knew.

The waitress came and took their orders. A light breeze stirred the new leaves on the nearby trees. The smell of summer mixed with that of corn tortillas, the most wonderful smell of all, Allie thought. They sipped Mexican Cokes, munched on chips and salsa to the sound of Latin music playing in the background and Allie felt herself begin to relax.

"I wasn't going to bring this up," Belinda said, "but you know that psychic that I've seen off and on?"

Allie fought not to roll her eyes.

"I know you say you don't believe in this stuff, but she said something interesting when I mentioned you."

"You told her about *me?*" Allie hadn't meant for her voice to rise so high. Her daughter looked over. She smiled at Nat and quickly changed her tone. "I really don't want you talking to anyone about me, let alone a…" She tried to come up with a word other than *charlatan*.

Belinda leaned forward, unfazed. "She thinks what's happening to you is because of guilt. Simply put, you feel guilty and it is manifesting itself into these…*incidents*."

Allie stared at her. Leave it to Belinda to get right to the heart of it.

Her friend lowered her voice as if afraid Nat might be listening. "It makes sense, if you think about it. Nick didn't know you were—" she glanced at Nat "—leaving him and going to file for custody of you-know-who, but *you* did know your plan. Then he goes and gets himself…" She grimaced in place of the word *killed.* "Something like that has to mess with your mind."

"Yes, losing your husband does mess with your mind no matter what kind of marriage you had." Fortunately, the waitress brought their food. Allie called Nat up to the table and, for a few moments, they ate in silence.

"The thing is…" Belinda said between bites.

"Can't we just enjoy our meal?" Allie pleaded.

Her friend waved that suggestion away, but didn't say more until they had finished and Nat had gone back to the play area.

"The psychic thinks there is more to it," Belinda said. "What if Nick *knew* about your…plan?"

"What are you saying?"

"Come on. You've been over Nick for a long time. His death wouldn't make you crazy—"

"I'm not crazy," she protested weakly.

"But what if he *did* know or at least suspected? Come on, Allie. We both know it was so not like Nick to go hunting up into the mountains alone, knowing that the grizzlies were eating everything they could get their paws on before hibernation." She didn't seem to notice Allie wince. "Didn't the ranger say Nick had food in his backpack?"

"He didn't take food to attract a bear, if that's what you're saying. He planned to stay a few days so of course he had food in his backpack."

"I'm not trying to upset you. But if he went up there to end it all, that was his choice. You can't go crazy because you feel guilty."

Her stomach turned at the thought of the backpack she'd been asked to identify. It had been shredded by the grizzly's claws. She'd been horrified to think of what the bear had done to Nick. She would never forget the officer who'd brought her the news.

"From what we've been able to assess at the scene, your husband was attacked by a grizzly and given the tracks and other signs—"

"Signs?"

"Blood, ma'am."

She'd had to sit down. "You're telling me he's…dead?"

"It certainly looks that way," the ranger said. Four days later, the search for Nick Taylor was called off because a winter storm had come in and it was believed that there was little chance he could have survived such an attack without immediate medical attention.

"Nick wouldn't," she managed to say now. In her heart of hearts, the man she knew so well, the man she'd been married to for more than six years, wouldn't purposely go into the woods with a plan to be killed by a grizzly.

But Nick had always been unpredictable. Moody and often depressed, too. The construction business hadn't been doing well even before Nick's death. What would he have done if he'd known she was leaving him and taking his daughter? Hadn't she been suspicious when Nick told her of his plan to go hunting alone? She'd actually thought he might be having an affair and wanted to spend a few days with his mistress. She'd actually hoped that was the case.

"You're going by yourself?" she'd asked. Nick couldn't even watch football by himself.

"I know things haven't been great with us lately," he'd said. That alone had surprised her. She really thought Nick hadn't noticed or cared. "I think a few days apart is just what we both need. I can tell you aren't happy. I promise you there will be changes when I get back and maybe I'll even come home with a nice buck." He'd cupped her face in his hands. "I don't think you know what you mean to me, but I promise to show you when I get back." He'd kissed her then, softly, sweetly, and for a moment, she'd wondered if Nick could change.

"You're wrong about Nick," she said now to Belinda. "If he was going to end it, he would have chosen the least painful way to do it. Not one—" she looked at Nat, who was swinging nearby, humming to herself and seemingly oblivious to their conversation "—that chose him. He had a gun with him he could have used."

"Maybe he didn't get the chance, but you're probably right," Belinda said and grabbed the check. "Let me get this. I didn't mean to upset you. It's just that you need to get a handle on whatever's been going on with you for you-know-who's sake." She cut her eyes to Nat, who headed toward them as they stood to leave.

"You're right about the guilt, though," Allie said, giving her friend that. She'd known as she'd watched Nick leave that day to go up into the mountains that nothing could change him enough to make her stay. She was going to ask him for a divorce when he came back.

Belinda changed the subject. "I saw your brother-in-law, Drew, earlier on the ranch."

Allie nodded. "He mentioned he was working up there. His construction company built the guest cabins."

"I'd forgotten that." Belinda frowned. "I was talking to Lily about photos at the rehearsal dinner. Did you know that Sarah is one of her bridesmaids?"

"My sister-in-law worked with Lily one season at her brother James's Canyon Bar." Allie had the impression that Lily didn't have a lot of female friends. Most of the math professors she knew were male, apparently. "I think James feels sorry for Sarah and you know Lily, she is so sweet."

"I have to hand it to Sarah, putting up with her mother day in and day out," Belinda said.

Allie didn't want to think about it. Along with fewer incidents the past few days, she'd also been blessed with no visits from her mother-in-law and Sarah.

"Sarah's a saint, especially—" Belinda lowered her voice

"—the way Mildred treats her. She is constantly bugging her about her weight and how she is never going to get a husband… It's awful."

Allie agreed.

"I don't understand why she doesn't leave."

"Where would she go and what would she do?" Allie said. "Sarah was in college when Mildred broke her leg. She quit to come home and take care of her mother. Mildred has milked it ever since. It used to annoy Nick, Sarah living in the guesthouse. He thought Sarah was taking advantage of his mother."

"Ha, it's the other way around. Sarah is on twenty-four-hour call. She told me that her mother got her out of bed at 2:00 a.m. one time to heat her some milk because she couldn't sleep. I would have put a pillow over the old nag's face."

Allie laughed and changed the subject. "You look especially nice today," she commented, realizing that her friend had seemed happier lately. It dawned on her why. "There's someone new in your life."

Belinda shrugged. She didn't like to talk about the men she dated because she thought it would jinx things for her. Not talking about them didn't seem to work, either, though. Belinda was so superstitious. Why else would she see a psychic to find out her future?

"This is going to be so much fun, the two of us working together again. Don't worry. I won't get in your way." Belinda took her hand. "I'm sorry I upset you. Sometimes I don't have the brains God gave a rock."

She didn't think that was the way the expression went, but said nothing. Belinda could be so…annoying and yet so sweet. Allie didn't know what she would have done without her the past few years. Belinda had been the only person she would talk freely to about Nick and the trouble between them.

"I'm just worried about you, honey," Belinda said, squeezing her hand. "I really think you should see someone—"

"I don't need a shrink."

"Not a shrink. Someone more…spiritual who can help you make sense of the things that you say keep happening."

"Things *do* keep happening," she snapped. "I'm not making them up."

"So talk to this woman," Belinda said just as adamantly. She pressed a business card into Allie's hand.

She glanced at it and groaned. "Your psychic friend?"

"She might be the *only* person who can help you," Belinda said cryptically. She gripped Allie's hand tighter. "She says she can get you in touch with Nick so you can get past this."

Allie stared at her for a moment before laughing out loud. "You have got to be kidding. What does she use? A Ouija board?"

"Don't laugh. This woman can tell you things that will make the hair on your head stand straight up."

That's all I need, she thought, reminded of Jackson Cardwell asking her if she was superstitious.

"Call her," Belinda said, closing Allie's fingers around the woman's business card. "You need closure, Allie. This woman can give it to you. She's expecting your call."

"I've been expecting your call, as well," said a sharp, older voice.

They both turned to see Mildred and her daughter. From the looks on their faces, they'd been standing there for some time.

Chapter Three

"Want to see the building for Montana's first Texas Boys Barbecue?" Tag asked after they'd dropped Jackson and Ford's luggage off at the small cabin on the side of the mountain and gone down to meet cousin Dana and her brood.

Dana Cardwell Savage was just as Tag had described her. Adorable and sweet and delighted that everyone was coming for the wedding.

"How is your cabin?" she asked after introducing him to her children with husband, Marshal Hud Savage. Hank was the spitting image of his father, Dana said, and six now. Mary was five and looked just like her mom. Then there were the twins, Angus and Brick, just a year and a half old with the same dark hair and eyes as all the Cardwells.

"The cabin is great," Jackson said as Ford instantly bonded with his second cousins. "Thank you so much for letting me stay there."

"Family is why we had them built," Dana said. "My Texas cousins will always have a place to stay when you visit. Or until you find a place to live in Montana when you realize you want to live up here," she added with a wink. "Isn't that right, Tag?"

"I would love to visit, but I'm never leaving Texas," Jackson said.

"Never say never," Tag commented under his breath.

"I was just about to take him down to see the restaurant location."

Ford took off with the other kids into a room full of toys and didn't even look back as his father left. Jackson almost felt as if he were losing his son to Montana and the Cardwell clan.

"Are you sure you don't want to wait until everyone gets here?" he asked as they left.

"Hayes and Laramie are flying in tomorrow. I was hoping you would pick them up at the airport. Austin is apparently on a case tying up some loose ends." He shrugged. Of the five of them, Austin was the loner. He was dedicated to his job and being tied up on a case was nothing new. "Anyway, it's your opinion I want. You're better at this than all three of them put together."

"So you haven't heard from Austin on the deal," Jackson guessed.

Tag shook his head. "You know how he is. He'll go along with whatever everyone else says. Come on," he said with a laugh when Jackson groaned. "I really do want your opinion."

"*Honest* opinion?" Jackson asked.

"Of course."

Jackson glanced around as they drove out of the ranch and down the highway to the turnoff to Big Sky. Being the youngest, he didn't remember anything about Montana. He'd been a baby when his mother had packed up her five sons and taken them to Texas.

Big Sky looked more like a wide spot in the road rather than a town. There were clusters of buildings broken only by sagebrush or golf greens.

"This is the lower Meadow Village," Tag told him. "There is also the Mountain Village higher up the mountain where the ski resort is. You really have to see this place in the winter. It's crazy busy around the holidays. There are a lot of second homes here so the residents fly in and spend a few weeks generally in the summer and the holidays. More and more people, though, are starting to live here year-round. There is opportunity here, Jackson."

Jackson wanted to tell his brother that he didn't need to sell him. He'd go along with whatever the others decided. In fact, he'd already spoken to Hayes about it. Once Hayes got on board, it was clear to Jackson that this was probably a done deal. The holdout, if there was one, would be Austin and only because he wouldn't be available to sign off on the deal. Even Laramie sounded as if he thought the restaurant was a good idea.

"Where does Harlan live?" Jackson asked as they drove past mansions, condos and some tiny old cabins that must have been there before anyone even dreamed of a Big Sky. He had only a vague recollection of his father from those few times Harlan had visited Texas when he was growing up.

"He lives in one of those cabins back there, the older ones. We can stop by his place if you like. More than likely he and Uncle Angus are down at the Corral Bar. It's their favorite watering hole. Maybe we could have a beer with them later."

"I'm sure I'll see him soon enough." Harlan was a stranger who hadn't even made Jackson's wedding, not that the marriage had lasted long, anyway. But he felt no tie to the man who'd fathered him and doubted he ever would. It was only when he thought about Ford that he had regrets. It would have been nice for Ford to have a grandfather. His ex-wife's family had no interest in Ford. So the only family his son had in Texas was Jackson's mother, Rosalee Cardwell and his brother Laramie. Tag had already moved to Montana and Hayes would be moving here soon.

"I'm getting to know Dad," Tag said. "He's pretty remarkable."

"Tell me about your wedding planner," Jackson said,

changing the subject then regretting the topic he'd picked when his brother grinned over at him. "I'm just curious about her." He hadn't told anyone about the cat or the terrified woman he'd found in the barn earlier. Her reaction seemed over the top given it had only been a cat. Though it *had* been a black one. Maybe she *was* superstitious.

"Allie's great. Dana suggested her. That's our Dana, always trying to help those in need. Allie lost her husband eight months ago. Terrible thing. He was hunting in the mountains and apparently killed by a grizzly bear."

"Apparently?"

"They never found his body. They think the bear dragged the body off somewhere. Won't be the first time remains have turned up years later in the mountains—if they turn up at all. They found his backpack and enough blood that he can be declared legally dead but I guess the insurance company has been dragging its feet."

Jackson thought of Allie and her little girl, Nat. "How horrible for them."

"Yeah, she's been having a hard time both emotionally and financially according to Dana, who suggested her for our wedding planner because of it. But Lily loves Allie and, of course, Natalie. That little girl is so darned bright."

"Yeah, Ford is definitely taken with her." But his thoughts were on Allie and her reaction to the cat flying out of that box of wedding decorations. It must have scared her half out of her wits in the emotional state she was in. "That was nice of Dana to hire her."

"Allie worked as a wedding planner before she married Nick Taylor. Dana offered Allie and Nat one of the new guest ranch cabins where we're staying. But I guess she thinks it would be better for Natalie to stay in their own home."

"Where do Allie and her daughter live now?"

"An old cabin down by the river. I'll show you on the

way back." Tag swung into a small complex and turned off the engine. "Welcome to the site of the next Texas Boys Barbecue joint."

"I THOUGHT YOU had a job," Mildred said to Allie over the sound of brass horns playing cantina music at the Mexican café.

"They allow lunch breaks," she said. "But I really need to get back." She excused herself to go to the ladies' room.

Mildred turned to Natalie, leaned down and pinched her cheek. "How is my sweetie today? Grandma misses you. When are you coming to my house?"

In the restroom, Allie splashed cold water on her face and tried to calm down. How much had they heard?

Enough that they had been looking at her strangely. Or was that all in her mind, as well? But if they heard Belinda trying to get her to see a psychic so she could reach Nick on the other side... Allie could well imagine what they would think.

She hurried, not wanting to leave Natalie with her grandmother for long. She hated it, but Mildred seemed to nag the child all the time about not spending enough time with her.

Leaving the restroom, she saw that Sarah and her mother hadn't taken a seat. Instead, they were standing at the takeout counter. There was no avoiding talking to them again.

"I couldn't help but overhear your...friend suggesting you see a...psychic?" Mother Taylor said, leaving no doubt that they had been listening. "Surely she meant a psychiatrist, which indicates that you are still having those hallucinations." She quirked an eyebrow, waiting for an answer.

"Belinda was only joking. I'm feeling much better, thank you."

Mildred's expression said she wasn't buying a minute of it. "Sarah, I left my sweater in the car."

"I'll get it, Mother." Sarah turned and headed for their vehicle parked out front.

"How is this…job of yours going?" Mildred asked. "I've never understood what wedding planners do."

Allie had actually told her once, listing about fifty things she did but Mildred clearly hadn't been listening.

"I'll have to tell you sometime," she said now. "But I need to get back to it. Come on, Natalie."

"You should let me have her for the rest of the day," Mildred said. "In fact, she can spend the night at my house."

"I'm sorry, but Natalie is getting horseback riding lessons this afternoon," Allie lied. "She's having a wonderful time with Dana's children."

"Well, she can still—"

"Not only that, I also prefer to have Nat with me right now. It's hard enough without Nick." Another lie followed by the biggest truth of all, "I need my daughter right now."

Mildred looked surprised. "That's the first time I've heard you mention my Nicky in months." She seemed about to cry. Sarah returned with her sweater, slipping it around her shoulders without even a thank-you from Mildred.

Nearby, Belinda was finishing up their bill.

"I really should get back to work." Allie tried to step past her mother-in-law, but the older woman grabbed her arm. "I worry that you are ill-equipped to take care of yourself, let alone a child. I need Natalie more than you do. I—"

Allie jerked her arm free. "Natalie would be heartbroken if she was late to her horseback riding lesson." She hurried to her daughter, picked up her purse off the table and, taking Nat's hand, left the restaurant, trying hard not to run.

She told herself to calm down. Any sign of her being upset and her in-laws would view it as her being unable to take care of Nat. But all she wanted was to get away and as quickly as possible.

But as she and Nat reached her van and she dug in her

purse for her keys, she realized they weren't there. Her heart began to pound. Since Nick's death, she was constantly losing her keys, her purse, her sunglasses…her mind.

"Forgetfulness is very common after a traumatic event," the doctor had told her when she'd gotten an appointment at her in-laws' insistence.

"It scares me. I try to remind myself where I put things so this doesn't happen, but when I go back to get whatever it was…I'm always so positive that's where I left it. Instead, I find it in some…strange place I could never imagine."

The doctor had chuckled and pulled out his prescription pad. "How are you sleeping?" He didn't even wait for her to answer. "I think once you start sleeping through the night, you're going to find that these instances of forgetfulness will go away."

The pills had only made it worse, though, she thought now as she frantically searched for her van keys. She could feel Nat watching her, looking worried. Sometimes it felt as if her five-year-old was taking care of her instead of the other way around.

"It's okay, sweetheart. Mama just misplaced her keys. I'm sure they're in here…."

"Looking for these?" The young waitress from the café came out the door, holding up her keys.

"Where did you find them?" Allie asked, thinking they must have fallen out of her purse at the table and ended up on the floor. That could happen to anyone.

"In the bathroom sink."

Allie stared at her.

"You must have dropped them while you were washing your hands," the young woman said with a shrug as she handed them over.

As if that was likely. She hadn't even taken her purse to

the restroom, had she? But she had it now and she couldn't remember. She'd been so upset to see Sarah and Mildred.

"Nat, what was Grandmother saying to you in the restaurant?"

"She wanted me to go to her house but I told her I couldn't. I'm going horseback riding when we get to the ranch," Nat announced. "Dana is taking me and the other kids." Her lower lip came out for a moment. "Grandma said she was really sad I wasn't going with her."

"Yes," Allie said as, with trembling fingers, she opened the van door. Tears stung her eyes. "But today is a happy day so *we* aren't going to be sad, right? There are lots of other days that you can spend with your grandmother." Nat brightened as she strapped her into her seat.

Just a few more minutes and she and Nat would be out of here. But as she started the van, she looked up to find Mother Taylor watching her from beside Sarah's pearl-white SUV. It was clear from her expression that she'd witnessed the lost-key episode.

From the front steps of the restaurant, Belinda waved then made the universal sign to telephone.

Allie knew Belinda didn't mean call her. Reaching in her pocket, she half expected the psychic's business card to be missing. But it was still there, she realized with sagging relief. As crazy as the idea of reaching Nick beyond the grave was, she'd do *anything* to make this stop.

WHEN ALLIE AND her daughter returned, Jackson was watching her from inside his cousin's two-story ranch house.

"She lost her husband some months back," Dana said, joining him at the window.

"I wasn't—"

"He went up into the mountains during hunting season," she continued, ignoring his attempt to deny he'd been wondering about Allie. "They found his backpack and his rifle and grizzly tracks."

"Tag mentioned it." Tag had pointed out Allie's small, old cabin by the river on their way back to the ranch. It looked as if it needed work. Hadn't Tag mentioned that her husband was in construction? "Tag said they never found her husband's body."

Dana shook her head. "But Nick's backpack was shredded and his rifle was half-buried in the dirt with grizzly tracks all around it. When he didn't show up after a few days and they had no luck finding him…"

"His remains will probably turn up someday," Hud said as he came in from the kitchen. Dana's husband, Hud, was the marshal in the canyon—just as his father had been before him. "About thirty years ago now, a hiker found a human skeleton of a man. He still hasn't been identified so who knows how long he'd been out there in the mountains."

"That must make it even harder for her," Jackson said.

"It was one reason I was so glad when she decided to take the job as wedding planner."

He watched Allie reappear to get a box out of the van. She seemed nervous, even upset. He wondered if something had happened at lunch. Now at least he understood why she had overreacted with the black cat.

Hud kissed his wife, saying he had to get back to work, leaving Dana and Jackson alone.

"Our fathers are setting up their equipment on the bandstand in the barn," Dana said. "Have you seen Harlan yet?"

"No," Jackson admitted. "Guess there is no time like the present, huh?"

Jackson hadn't seen his father in several years, and even then Harlan hadn't seemed to know how to act around him—or his other sons, for that matter. As they entered the barn, Tag joining them, he saw his father and uncle standing on the makeshift stage, guitars in their hands, and was surprised when he remembered a song his father had once sung to him.

He didn't know how old he'd been at the time, but he recalled Harlan coming into his bedroom one night in Texas and playing a song on his guitar for him. He remembered being touched by the music and his father's voice.

On stage, the two brothers began playing their guitars in earnest. His father began singing. It was the voice Jackson remembered and it was like being transported back to his childhood. It rattled him more than he wanted to admit. He'd thought he and his father had no connection. But just hearing Harlan sing made him realize that he'd been lying to himself about not only the lack of connection, but also his need for it.

Harlan suddenly broke off at the sight of his sons. He stared through the dim barn for a moment, then put down his guitar to bound off the stage and come toward Jackson. He seemed young and very handsome, belying his age, Jackson thought. A man in his prime.

"Jackson," he said, holding out his hand. His father's hand was large and strong, the skin dry, callused and warm. "Glad you made it. So where are the rest of your brothers?"

"They're supposed to fly in tomorrow. At least Laramie and Hayes are," Tag said. "Austin... Well, he said he would do his best to make it. He's tied up on a case, but I'm sure you know how that goes." At Christmas, Tag had found out what their father did besides drink beer and play guitar—and shared that amazing news with them. Both Harlan and his brother Angus had worked undercover as government agents and still might, even though they were reportedly retired.

"Duty calls sometimes," Harlan agreed. "I'm glad I'm retired."

"Until the next time someone gets into trouble and needs help," Tag said.

Harlan merely smiled in answer.

Jackson was glad to see that his brother and their father could joke. Tag, being the oldest, remembered the years living in Montana and their father more than his brothers.

"The old man isn't so bad," Tag had told them after his visit at Christmas. "He's starting to grow on me."

Jackson had laughed, but he'd been a little jealous. He would love for his son to have a grandfather. He couldn't imagine, though, how Harlan could be a part of his only grandson's life, even if he wanted to. Texas and Montana were just too far apart. And Harlan probably had no interest, anyway.

"Where's that bride-to-be?" Uncle Angus asked Tag as he hopped off the stage and came toward them.

"Last minute preparations for the wedding," Tag said. "You can't believe the lists she's made. It's the mathematician in her. She's so much more organized than I am. Which reminds me, Jackson and I have to drive down to Bozeman to pick up the rings."

"It took a wedding to get you Cardwell boys to Montana, I see." Uncle Angus threw an arm around Jackson. "So how are you liking it up here? I saw that boy of yours. Dana's got him riding horses already. You're going to have one devil of a time getting him to go back to Texas after this."

Didn't Jackson know it. He'd hardly seen his son all day. Even now Ford had been too busy to give Jackson more than a quick wave from the corral where he'd been with the kids and the hired man, Walker.

"Ford is going to sleep like a baby tonight after all this fresh air, sunshine and high altitude," Jackson said. "He's not the only one," he added with a laugh.

"It's good for him," Harlan said. "I was talking to him earlier. He's taken with that little girl."

"Like father like son," Tag said under his breath as Allie came in from the back of the barn.

Jackson saw her expression. "I think I'd better go check on my son," he said as he walked toward Allie. He didn't have time to think about what he was about to do. He moved to her, taking her arm and leading her back out of the barn. "What's wrong?"

For a moment she looked as if she were going to deny anything was. But then tears filled her eyes. He walked her around the far side of the barn. He could hear Dana out by the corral instructing the kids in horseback riding lessons. Inside the barn, his father and uncle struck up another tune.

"It's nothing, really," she said and brushed at her tears. "I've been so forgetful lately. I didn't remember that the band would be setting up this afternoon."

He saw that she held a date book in her trembling hand.

"It wasn't written down in your date book?"

She glanced at her book. "It was but for some reason I marked it out."

"No big deal, right?"

"It's just that I don't remember doing it."

He could see that she was still upset and wondered if there wasn't something more going on. He reminded himself that Allie had lost her husband only months ago. Who knew what kind of emotional roller coaster that had left her on.

"You need to cut yourself more slack," he said. "We all forget things."

She nodded, but he could see she was still worried. No, not worried, scared. He thought of the black cat and had a feeling it hadn't been her first scare like that.

"I feel like such a fool," she said.

Instinctively, he put his arm around her. "Give yourself time. It's going to be all right."

She looked so forlorn that taking her in his arms seemed not only the natural thing to do at that moment, but the only thing to do under the circumstances. At first she felt board-stiff in his arms, then after a moment she seemed to melt into him. She buried her face into his chest as if he were an anchor in a fierce storm.

Suddenly, she broke the embrace and stepped back. He followed her gaze to one of the cabins on the mountainside behind him and the man standing there.

"Who is that?" he asked, instantly put off by the scowling man.

"My brother-in-law, Drew. He's doing some repairs on the ranch. He and Nick owned a construction company together. They built the guest cabins."

The man's scowl had turned into a cold stare. Jackson saw Allie's reaction. "We weren't doing anything wrong."

She shook her head as the man headed down the mountainside to his pickup parked in the pines. "He's just very protective." Allie looked as if she had the weight of the world on her shoulders again.

Jackson watched her brother-in-law slowly drive out of the ranch. Allie wasn't the only one the man was glaring at.

"I need to get back inside," she said and turned away.

He wanted to go after her. He also wanted to put his fist into her brother-in-law's face. *Protective my butt,* he thought. He wanted to tell Allie to ignore all of it. Wanted... Hell, that was just it. He didn't know what he wanted at the moment. Even if he did, he couldn't have it. He warned himself to stay away from Allie Taylor. Far away. He was only here for the wedding. While he felt for the woman, he couldn't help her.

"There you are," Tag said as he came up behind them. "Ready to go with me to Bozeman to get the rings?"

Jackson glanced toward the barn door Allie was stepping through. "Ready."

Chapter Four

As Jackson started to leave with his brother, he turned to look back at the barn. Just inside the door he saw Allie. All his survival instincts told him to keep going, but his mother had raised a Texas cowboy with a code of honor. Or at least she'd tried. Something was wrong and he couldn't walk away.

"Give me just a minute," he said and ran back. As he entered the barn, he saw Allie frantically searching for something in the corner of the barn. His father and brother were still playing at the far end, completely unaware of them.

"What are you looking for?"

She seemed embarrassed that he'd caught her. He noticed that she'd gone pale and looked upset. "I know I put my purse right there with my keys in it."

He glanced at the empty table. "Maybe it fell under it." He bent down to look under the red-and-white-checked tablecloth. "The barn is looking great, by the way. You've done a beautiful job."

She didn't seem to hear him. She was moving from table to table, searching for her purse. He could see that she was getting more anxious by the moment. "I know I put it right there so I wouldn't forget it when I left."

"Here it is," Jackson said as he spied what he assumed had to be her purse not on a table, but in one of the empty boxes that had held the decorations.

She rushed to him and took the purse and hurriedly looked inside, pulling out her keys with obvious relief.

"You would have found it the moment you started loading the boxes into your van," he said, seeing that she was still shaken.

She nodded. "Thank you. I'm not usually like this."

"No need to apologize. I hate losing things. It drives me crazy."

She let out a humorless laugh. "Crazy, yes." She took a deep breath and let it out slowly. Tears welled in her eyes.

"Hey, it's okay."

He wanted to comfort her, but kept his distance after what had happened earlier. "It really is okay."

She shook her head as the music stopped and quickly wiped her eyes, apologizing again. She looked embarrassed and he wished there was something he could say to put her at ease.

"Earlier, I was just trying to comfort you. It was just a hug," he said.

She met his gaze. "One I definitely needed. You have been so kind...."

"I'm not kind."

She laughed and shook her head. "Are you always so self-deprecating?"

"No, just truthful."

"Well, thank you." She clutched the keys in her hand as if afraid she would lose them if she let them out of her sight.

At the sound of people approaching, she stepped away from him.

"Let me load those boxes in your van. I insist," he said before she could protest.

As Dana, Lily and the kids came through the barn door they stopped to admire what Allie had accomplished. There were lots of oohs and ahhs. But it was Lily whose face lit up as she took in the way the barn was being transformed.

Jackson shifted his gaze to Allie's face as she humbly accepted their praise. Dana introduced Jackson to Lily. He could see right away why his brother had fallen for the woman.

"Please come stay at one of the guest cabins for the rest of the wedding festivities," Dana was saying to Allie.

"It is so generous of you to offer the cabin," Allie said, looking shocked at the offer.

"Not at all. It will make it easier for you so you don't have to drive back and forth. Also I'm being selfish. The kids adore Natalie. It will make the wedding a lot more fun for them."

Allie, clearly fighting tears of gratitude, said she would think about it. Jackson felt his heartstrings pulled just watching. "I'll work hard to make this wedding as perfect as it can be. I won't let you down."

Lily gave her a hug. "Allie, it's already perfect!"

Jackson was surprised that Lily McCabe had agreed to a Western wedding. According to the lowdown he'd heard, Lily taught mathematics at Montana State University. She'd spent her younger years at expensive boarding schools after having been born into money.

Jackson wondered if the woman had ever even been on a horse—before she met the Cardwells. Apparently, Allie was worried that a Western wedding was the last thing a woman like Lily McCabe would want.

"Are you sure this is what *you* want?" Allie asked Lily. "After all, it is *your* wedding."

Lily laughed. "Just to see the look on my parents' faces will make it all worthwhile." At Allie's horrified look, she quickly added, "I'm kidding. Though that is part of it. But when you marry into the Cardwell family, you marry into ranching and all that it comes with. I want this wedding to be a celebration of that.

"This is going to be the best wedding ever," Lily said as

she looked around the barn. "Look at me," she said, holding out her hands. "I'm actually shaking I'm so excited." She stepped to Allie and gave her another hug. "Thank you so much."

Allie appeared taken aback for a moment by Lily's sudden show of affection. The woman really was becoming more like the Cardwells every day. Or at least Dana Cardwell. That wasn't a bad thing, he thought.

"We should probably talk about the other arrangements. When is your final dress fitting?"

"Tomorrow. The dress is absolutely perfect, and the boots!" Lily laughed. "I'm so glad Dana suggested red boots. I love them!"

This was going to be like no wedding Allie had ever planned, Jackson thought. The Cardwells went all out, that was for sure.

He looked around the barn, seeing through the eyes of the guests who would be arriving for the wedding. Allie had found a wonderful wedding cake topper of a cowboy and his bride dancing that was engraved with the words: *For the rest of my life.* Tag had said that Lily had cried when she'd seen it.

The cake was a little harder to nail, according to Tag. Jackson mentally shook his head at even the memory of his brother discussing wedding cakes with him. Apparently, there were cake designs resembling hats and boots, covered wagons and cowhide, lassoes and lariats, spurs and belt buckles and horses and saddles. Some cakes had a version of all of them, which he could just imagine would have thrown his brother for a loop, he thought now, grinning to himself.

"I like simple better," Lily had said when faced with all the options. "It's the mathematician in me."

Allie had apparently kept looking until she found what she thought might be the perfect one. It was an elegant white, frosted, tiered cake with white roses and ribbons in a similar design as Lily's Western wedding dress.

"I love it," Lily had gushed. "It's perfect."

They decided on white roses and daisies for her bouquet. Bouquets of daisies would be on each of the tables, the vases old boots, with the tables covered with red-checked cloths and matching napkins.

Jackson's gaze returned to Allie. She seemed to glow under the compliments, giving him a glimpse of the self-assured woman he suspected she'd been before the tragedy.

"Jackson?"

He turned to find Tag standing next to him, grinning.

"I guess you didn't hear me. Must have had your mind somewhere else." Tag glanced in Allie's direction and then wisely jumped back as Jackson took a playful swing at him as they left the barn.

"You sure waited until the last minute," Jackson said to his brother as they headed for Tag's vehicle. "Putting off the rings…" He shook his head. "You sure you want to go through with this?"

His brother laughed. "More sure than I have been about anything in my life. Come on, let's go."

"I'll see if Ford wants to come along," Jackson said. "I think that's enough cowboying for one day."

But when he reached the corral, he found his son wearing a straw Western hat and atop a huge horse. Jackson felt his pulse jump at the sight and his first instinct was to insist Ford get down from there right away.

But when he got a good look at his son's face, his words died on a breath. He'd never seen Ford this happy. His cheeks were flushed, his eyes bright. He looked…proud.

"Look at me," he called to his father.

All Jackson could do was nod as his son rode past him. He was incapable of words at that moment.

"Don't worry about your son," his father said as he joined him at the corral fence. "I'll look after him until you get back."

ALLIE LISTENED TO Jackson and Tag joking with each other as they left the barn. Jackson Cardwell must think her the most foolish woman ever, screaming over nothing more than a cat, messing up her date book and panicking because she'd misplaced her purse.

But what had her still upset was the hug. It had felt so good to be in Jackson's arms. It had been so long since anyone had held her like that. She'd felt such an overwhelming need...

And then Drew had seen them. She'd been surprised by the look on his face. He'd seemed...angry and upset as if she was cheating on Nick. Once this investigation was over, maybe they could all put Nick to rest. In the meantime, she just hoped Drew didn't go to his mother with this.

Instinctively, she knew that Jackson wouldn't say anything. Not about her incidents or about the hug.

Dana announced she was taking the kids down to the house for naptime. Allie could tell that Nat had wanted to go down to the house—but for lemonade and cookies. Nat probably needed a nap, as well, but Allie couldn't take her up to the cabin right now. She had work to do if she hoped to have the barn ready for the rehearsal dinner tomorrow night.

"I really need your help," she told her daughter. Nat was always ready to give a helping hand. Well, she was before the Cardwell Ranch and all the animals, not to mention other kids to play with.

"Okay, Mama." She glanced back at the barn door wistfully, though. Nat had always wanted brothers and sisters, but they hadn't been in Allie's plans. She knew she could take care of one child without any help from Nick. He'd wanted a boy and insisted they try for another child soon after Nat was born.

Allie almost laughed. Guilt? She had so much of it where Nick and his family were concerned. She had wanted to enjoy her baby girl so she'd gone on the pill behind Nick's back. It had been more than dishonest. He would have killed her if he had found out. The more time that went by, the less she wanted another child with her husband so she'd stayed on the pill. Even Nick's tantrums about her not getting pregnant were easier to take than having another child with him.

She hadn't even told Belinda, which was good since her friend was shocked when she told her she was leaving Nick and moving far away.

"Divorcing him is one thing," Belinda had said. "But I don't see how you can keep his kid from him or keep Nat from his family."

"Nick wanted a son. He barely takes notice of Nat. The only time he notices her is when other people are around and then he plays too rough with her. When she cries, he tells her to toughen up."

"So you're going to ask for sole custody? Isn't Nick going to fight you?"

Allie knew it would be just like Nick to fight for Nat out of meanness and his family would back him up. "I'm going to move to Florida. I've already lined up a couple of jobs down there. They pay a lot more than here. I really doubt Nick will bother flying that far to see Nat—at least more than a few times."

"You really are going to leave him," Belinda had said. "When?"

"Soon." That had been late summer. She'd desperately wanted a new start. Nick would be occupied with hunting season in the fall so maybe he wouldn't put up much of a fight.

Had Belinda said something to Nick? Or had he just seen something in Allie that told him he had lost her?

"How can I help you, Mama?" Nat asked, dragging her from her thoughts.

Allie handed her daughter one end of a rope garland adorned with tiny lights in the shape of boots. "Let's string this up," she suggested. "And see how pretty it looks along the wall."

Nat's eyes lit up. "It's going to be beautiful," she said. *Beautiful* was her latest favorite word. To her, most everything was beautiful.

Allie yearned for that kind of innocence again—if she'd ever had it. But maybe she could find it for her daughter. She had options. She could find work anywhere as a wedding planner, but did she want to uproot her daughter from what little family she had? Nat loved her Uncle Drew and Sarah could be very sweet. Mildred, even as ungrandmotherly as she was, was Nat's only grandmother.

Allie tried to concentrate on her work. The barn was taking shape. She'd found tiny cowboy boot lights to put over the bar area. Saddles on milk cans had been pulled up to the bar for extra seating.

Beverages would be chilling in a metal trough filled with ice. Drinks would be served in Mason jars and lanterns would hang from the rafters for light. A few bales of hay would be brought in around the bandstand.

When they'd finished, Allie plugged in the last of the lights and Nat squealed with delight.

She checked her watch. "Come on," she told her daughter. "We've done enough today. We need to go into town for a few things. Tomorrow your aunt Megan will be coming to help." Nat clapped in response. She loved her auntie Megan, Allie's half sister.

After Allie's mother died, her father had moved away, remarried and had other children. Allie had lost touch with her father, as well as his new family. But about a year ago, her stepsister Megan had found her. Ten years younger, Megan was now twenty-three and a recent graduate in design. When she'd shown an interest in working on the Cardwell Ranch wedding, Allie had jumped at it.

"I really could use the help, but when can you come down?" Megan lived in Missoula and had just given her two weeks' notice at her job.

"Go ahead and start without me. I'll be there within a few days of the wedding. That should be enough time, shouldn't it?"

"Perfect," Allie had told her. "Natalie and I will start. I'll save the fun stuff for you." Natalie loved Megan, who was cute and young and always up for doing something fun with her niece.

The thought of Megan's arrival tomorrow had brightened Natalie for a moment, but Allie now saw her looking longingly at the Savage house.

"How about we have something to eat while we're in Bozeman?" Allie suggested.

Nat's eyes widened with new interest as she asked if they could go to her favorite fast-food burger place. The Taylors had introduced her daughter to fast food, something Allie had tried to keep at a minimum.

But this evening, she decided to make an exception. She loved seeing how happy her daughter was. Nat's cheeks were pink from the fresh air and sunshine.

All the way into town, she talked excitedly about the horses and the other kids. This wedding planner job at Cardwell Ranch was turning out to be a good thing for both of them, Allie thought as they drove home.

By the time they reached the cabin Nat had fallen asleep in her car seat and didn't even wake up when Allie parked out front. Deciding to take in the items she'd purchased first, then bring in her daughter, Allie stepped into the cabin and stopped dead.

At the end of the hall, light flickered. A candle. She hadn't lit a candle. Not since Nick. He liked her in candle-light. The smell of the candle and the light reminded her of the last time they'd had sex. Not made love. They hadn't made love since before Natalie was born.

As she started down the hallway, she told herself that she'd thrown all the candles away. Even if she'd missed one, she wouldn't have left a candle burning.

She stopped in the bedroom doorway. Nick's shirt was back, spread on the bed as if he were in it, lying there wait-ing for her. The smell of the sweet-scented candle made her nauseous. She fought the panicked need to run.

"Mama?" Nat's sleepy voice wavered with concern. "Did Daddy come back?" Not just concern. Anxiety. Nick scared her with his moodiness and surly behavior. Nat was smart. She had picked up on the tension between her parents.

Allie turned to wrap her arms around her daughter. The warmth of her five-year-old, Nat's breath on her neck, the solid feel of the ground under her feet, those were the things she concentrated on as she carried Natalie down the hall-way to her room.

Her daughter's room had always been her haven. It was the only room in the house that Nick hadn't cared what she did with. So she'd painted it sky-blue, adding white float-ing clouds, then trees and finally a river as green and sunlit as the one out Nat's window.

Nick had stuck his head in the door while she was paint-ing it. She'd seen his expression. He'd been impressed—and he hadn't wanted to be—before he snapped, "You going to cook dinner or what?" He seemed to avoid the room after that, which was fine with her.

Now, she lay down on the bed with Nat. It had been her

daughter's idea to put stars on the ceiling, the kind that shone only at night with the lights out.

"I like horses," Nat said with a sigh. "Ms. Savage says a horse can tell your mood and that if you aren't in a good one, you'll get bucked off." She looked at her mother. "Do you think that's true?"

"I think if Ms. Savage says it is, then it is."

Nat smiled as if she liked the answer.

Allie could tell she was dog-tired, but fighting sleep.

"I'm going to ride Rocket tomorrow," Natalie said.

"Rocket? That sounds like an awfully fast horse." She saw that Nat's eyelids had closed. She watched her daughter sleep for a few moments, then eased out of bed.

After covering her, she opened the window a few inches to let the cool summer night air into the stuffy room. Spending time with her daughter made her feel better, but also reminded her how important it was that she not let anyone know about the things that had been happening to her.

She thought of Jackson Cardwell and the black cat that had somehow gotten into her box of decorations. She hadn't imagined that. She smiled to herself. Such a small thing and yet...

This time, she went straight to her bedroom, snuffed out the candle and opened the window, thankful for the breeze that quickly replaced the sweet, cloying scent with the fresh night air.

On the way out of the room, she grabbed Nick's shirt and took both the shirt and the candle to the trash, but changed her mind. Dropping only the candle in the trash, she took the shirt over to the fireplace. Would burning Nick's favorite shirt mean she was crazy?

Too bad, she thought as she dropped the shirt on the grate and added several pieces of kindling and some newspaper. Allie hesitated for only a moment before lighting the paper with a match. It caught fire, crackling to life and forcing her to step back. She watched the blaze destroy the shirt and reached for the poker, determined that not a scrap of it would be left.

She had to get control of her life. She thought of Jackson Cardwell and his kindness. He had no idea how much it meant to her.

As she watched the flames take the last of Nick's shirt, she told herself at least this would be the last she'd see of that blamed shirt.

Chapter Five

Jackson met Hayes and Laramie at the airport, but while it was good to see them, he was distracted.

They talked about the barbecue restaurant and Harlan and the wedding before McKenzie showed up while they were waiting for their luggage to pick up Hayes. Hayes had been in Texas tying up things with the sale of his business.

Jackson had heard their relationship was serious, but seeing McKenzie and Hayes together, he saw just how serious. Another brother falling in love in Montana, he thought with a shake of his head. Hayes and McKenzie would be joining them later tonight at the ranch for dinner.

He and Laramie ended up making the drive to Cardwell Ranch alone. Laramie talked about the financial benefits of the new barbecue restaurant and Jackson tuned him out. He couldn't get his mind off Allie Taylor.

Maybe it was because he'd been through so much with his ex, but he felt like a kindred spirit. The woman was going through her own private hell. He wished there was something he could do.

"Are you listening?" Laramie asked.

"Sure."

"I forget how little interest my brothers have in the actual running of this corporation."

"Don't let it hurt your feelings. I just have something else on my mind."

"A woman."

"Why would you say that, knowing me?"

Laramie looked over at him. "I was joking. You swore off women after Juliet, right? At least that's what you... Wait a minute, has something changed?"

"Nothing." He said it too sharply, making his brother's eyebrow shoot up.

Laramie fell silent for a moment, but Jackson could feel him watching him out of the corner of his eye.

"Is this your first wedding since...you and Juliet split?" Laramie asked carefully.

Jackson shook his head at his brother's attempt at diplomacy. "It's not the wedding. There's this...person I met who I'm worried about."

"Ah. Is this person—"

"It's a woman, all right? But it isn't like that."

"Hey," Laramie said, holding up his hands. "I just walked in. If you don't want to tell me—"

"She lost her husband some months ago and she has a little girl the same age as Ford and she's struggling."

Laramie nodded. "Okay."

"She's the wedding planner."

His brother's eyebrow shot up again.

"I'll just be glad when this wedding is over," Jackson said and thought he meant it. "By the way, when is Mom flying in?" At his brother's hesitation, he demanded, "What's going on with Mom?"

ALLIE HAD UNPACKED more boxes of decorations by the time she heard a vehicle pull up the next morning. Natalie, who had been coloring quietly while her mother worked, went running when she spotted her aunt Megan. Allie smiled as Megan picked Nat up and swung her around, both of them laughing. It was a wonderful sound. Megan had a way with Natalie. Clearly, she loved kids.

"Sorry I'm so late, but I'm here and ready to go to work." Megan was dressed in a T-shirt, jeans and athletic shoes. She had taken after their father and had the Irish green eyes with the dark hair and complexion. She was nothing short of adorable, sweet and cute. "Wow, the barn is already looking great," she exclaimed as she walked around, Natalie holding her hand and beaming up at her.

"I helped Mama with the lights," Nat said.

"I knew it," Megan said. "I can see your handiwork." She grinned down at her niece. "Did I hear you can now ride a horse?"

Natalie quickly told her all about the horses, naming each as she explained how to ride a horse. "You have to hang on to the reins."

"I would imagine you do," Megan agreed.

"Maybe you can ride with us," Nat suggested.

"Maybe I can. But right now I need to help your mom."

Just then Dana stuck her head in the barn doorway and called to Natalie. Allie introduced Dana to her stepsister, then watched as her daughter scurried off for an afternoon ride with her friends. She gave a thankful smile to Dana as they left.

"Just tell me what to do," Megan said and Allie did, even more thankful for the help. They went to work on the small details Allie knew Megan would enjoy.

Belinda stopped by to say hello to Megan and give Allie an update on the photos. She'd met with Lily that morning, had made out a list of photo ideas and sounded excited.

Allie was surprised when she overheard Belinda and Megan discussing a recent lunch. While the three of them had spent some time together since Megan had come back into Allie's life, she hadn't known that Belinda and Megan had become friends.

She felt jealous. She knew it was silly. They were both

single and probably had more in common than with Allie, who felt as if she'd been married forever.

"How are you doing?" Megan asked after Belinda left.

"Fine."

"No, really."

Allie studied her stepsister for a moment. They'd become close, but she hadn't wanted to share what was going on. It was embarrassing and the fewer people who knew she was losing her mind the better, right?

"It's been rough." Megan didn't know that she had been planning to leave Nick. As far as her sister had known, Allie had been happily married. Now Allie regretted that she hadn't been more honest with Megan.

"But I'm doing okay now," she said as she handed Megan another gift bag to fill. "It's good to be working again. I love doing this." She glanced around the barn feeling a sense of satisfaction.

"Well, I'm glad I'm here now," Megan said. "This is good for Natalie, too."

Good for all of us, Allie thought.

JACKSON LOOKED AT his brother aghast. "Mom's dating?" He should have known that if their mom confided in anyone it would be Laramie. The sensible one, was what she called him, and swore that out of all her sons, Laramie was the only one who she could depend on to be honest with her.

Laramie cleared his throat. "It's a little more than dating. She's on her honeymoon."

"Her *what?*"

"She wanted it to be a surprise."

"Well, it sure as hell is that. Who did she marry?"

"His name is Franklin Wellington the Fourth. He's wealthy, handsome, very nice guy, actually."

"*You've* met him?"

"He and Mom are flying in just before the wedding on his private jet. It's bigger than ours."

"Laramie, I can't believe you would keep this from the rest of us, let alone that Mom would."

"She didn't want to take away from Tag's wedding but they had already scheduled theirs before Tag announced his." Laramie shrugged. "Hey, she's deliriously happy and hoping we will all be happy for her."

Jackson couldn't believe this. Rosalee Cardwell hadn't just started dating after all these years, she'd gotten married?

"I wonder how Dad will take it?" Laramie said. "We all thought Mom had been pining away for him all these years...."

"Maybe she was."

"Well, not anymore."

"BUT YOU *HAVE* to go on the horseback ride," Natalie cried.

As he stepped into the cool shade, Jackson saw Allie look around the barn for help, finding none. Hayes was off somewhere with his girlfriend, McKenzie, Tag was down by the river writing his vows, Lily was picking her parents up at the airport, Laramie had restaurant business and Hud was at the marshal's office, working. There had still been no word from Austin. Or their mother.

Wanting to spend some time with his son, Jackson had agreed to go on the short horseback ride with Dana and the kids that would include lunch on the mountain.

"Dana promised she would find you a very gentle horse, in other words, a really *old* one," Megan joked.

Natalie was doing her "please-Mama-please" face.

"Even my dad is going to ride," Ford said, making everyone laugh.

Allie looked at the boy. "Your dad is a cowboy."

Ford shook his head. "He can't even rope a cow. He tried

once at our neighbor's place and he was really bad at it. So it's okay if you're really bad at riding a horse."

Jackson smiled and ruffled his son's hair. "You really should come along, Allie."

"I have too much work to—"

"I will stay here and get things organized for tomorrow," Megan said. "No more arguments. Go on the ride with your daughter. Go." She shooed her toward the barn door.

"I guess I'm going on the horseback ride," Allie said. The kids cheered. She met Jackson's gaze as they walked toward the corral where Dana and her ranch hand, Walker, were saddling horses. "I've never been on a horse," she whispered confidentially to Jackson.

"Neither had your daughter and look at her now," he said as he watched Ford and Natalie saddle up. They both had to climb up the fence to get on their horses, but they now sat eagerly waiting in their saddles.

"I'll help you," Jackson said as he took Allie's horse's reins from Dana. He demonstrated how to get into the saddle then gave her a boost.

"It's so high up here," she said as she put her boot toes into the stirrups.

"Enjoy the view," Jackson said and swung up onto his horse.

They rode up the mountain, the kids chattering away, Dana giving instructions to them as they went.

After a short while, Jackson noticed that Allie seemed to have relaxed a little. She was looking around as if enjoying the ride and when they stopped in a wide meadow, he saw her patting her horse's neck and talking softly to it.

"I'm afraid to ask what you just said to your horse," he joked as he moved closer. Her horse had wandered over to some tall grass away from the others.

"Just thanking him for not bucking me off," she admitted shyly.

"Probably a good idea, but your horse is a she. A mare."

"Oh, hopefully, she wasn't insulted." Allie actually smiled. The afternoon sun lit her face along with the smile.

He felt his heart do a loop-de-loop. He tried to rein it back in as he looked into her eyes. That tantalizing green was deep and dark, inviting, and yet he knew a man could drown in those eyes.

Suddenly, Allie's horse shied. In the next second it took off as if it had been shot from a cannon. To her credit, she hadn't let go of her reins, but she grabbed the saddlehorn and let out a cry as the mare raced out of the meadow headed for the road.

Jackson spurred his horse and raced after her. He could hear the startled cries of the others behind him. He'd been riding since he was a boy, so he knew how to handle his horse. But Allie, he could see, was having trouble staying in the saddle with her horse at a full gallop.

He pushed his harder and managed to catch her, riding alongside until he could reach over and grab her reins. The horses lunged along for a moment. Next to him Allie started to fall. He grabbed for her, pulling her from her saddle and into his arms as he released her reins and brought his own horse up short.

Allie slid down his horse to the ground. He dismounted and dropped beside her. "Are you all right?"

"I think so. What happened?"

He didn't know. One minute her horse was munching on grass, the next it had taken off like a shot.

Jackson could see that she was shaken. She sat down on the ground as if her legs would no longer hold her. He could hear the others riding toward them. When Allie heard her daughter calling to her, she hurriedly got to her feet, clearly wanting to reassure Natalie.

"Wow, that was some ride," Allie said as her daughter came up.

"Are you all right?" Dana asked, dismounting and joining her.

"I'm fine, really," she assured her and moved to her daughter, still in the saddle, to smile up at her.

"What happened?" Dana asked Jackson.

"I don't know."

"This is a good spot to have lunch," Dana announced more cheerfully than Jackson knew she felt.

"I'll go catch the horse." He swung back up into the saddle and took off after the mare. "I'll be right back for lunch. Don't let Ford eat all the sandwiches."

ALLIE HAD NO idea why the horse had reacted like that. She hated that she was the one who'd upset everyone.

"Are you sure you didn't spur your horse?" Natalie asked, still upset.

"She isn't wearing spurs," Ford pointed out.

"Maybe a bee stung your horse," Natalie suggested.

Dana felt bad. "I wanted your first horseback riding experience to be a pleasant one," she lamented.

"It was. It is," Allie reassured her although in truth, she wasn't looking forward to getting back on the horse. But she knew she had to for Natalie's sake. The kids had been scared enough as it was.

Dana had spread out the lunch on a large blanket with the kids all helping when Jackson rode up, trailing her horse. The mare looked calm now, but Allie wasn't sure she would ever trust it again.

Jackson met her gaze as he dismounted. Dana was already on her feet, heading for him. Allie left the kids to join them.

"What is it?" Dana asked, keeping her voice down.

Jackson looked to Allie as if he didn't want to say in front of her.

"Did I do something to the horse to make her do that?" she asked, fearing that she had.

His expression softened as he shook his head. "You didn't do *anything.*" He looked at Dana. "Someone shot the mare." He moved so Dana could see the bloody spot on the horse. "Looks like a small caliber. Probably a .22. Fortunately, the shooter must have been some distance away or it could have been worse. The bullet barely broke the horse's hide. Just enough to spook the mare."

"We've had teenagers on four-wheelers using the old log-ging roads on the ranch," Dana said. "I heard shots a few days ago." Suddenly, all the color drained from Dana's face. "Allie could have been killed," she whispered. "Or one of the kids. When we get back, I'll call Hud."

JACKSON INSISTED ON riding right beside Allie on the way back down the mountain. He could tell that Allie had been happy to get off the horse once they reached the corral.

"Thank you for saving me," she said. "It seems like you keep doing that, doesn't it?" He must have looked panicked by the thought because she quickly added, "I'm fine now. I will try not to need saving again." She flashed him a smile and disappeared into the barn.

"Ready?" Tag said soon after Jackson had finished help-ing unsaddle the horses and put the tack away.

Dana had taken the kids down to the house to play, say-ing they all needed some downtime. He could tell that she was still upset and anxious to call Hud. "Don't forget the barbecue and dance tonight," she reminded him. "Then to-morrow is the bachelor party, right?"

Jackson groaned. He'd forgotten that Tag had been wait-ing for them all to arrive so they could have the party. The last thing he needed was a party. Allie's horse taking off like that… It had left him shaken, as well. Dana was convinced it had been teenagers who'd shot the horse. He hoped that was all it had been.

"Glad you're back," Tag said. "We're all going down to the Corral for a beer. Come on. At least four of us are here. We'll be back in time for dinner."

Ford was busy with the kids and Dana. "Are you sure he isn't too much?" Jackson asked his cousin. "I feel like I've been dumping him on you since we got here."

She laughed. "Are you kidding? My children adore having their cousin around. They've actually all been getting along better than usual. Go have a drink with your brothers. Enjoy yourself, Jackson. I suspect you get little time without Ford."

It was true. And yet he missed his son. He told himself again that he would be glad when they got back to Texas. But seeing how much fun Ford was having on the ranch, he doubted his son would feel the same.

ALLIE STARED AT her date book, heart racing. She'd been feeling off balance since her near-death experience on the horse. When she'd told Megan and Belinda about it on her return to the barn, they'd been aghast.

She'd recounted her tale right up to where Jackson had returned with the mare and the news that it had been shot.

"That's horrible," Megan said. "I'm so glad you didn't get bucked off. Was the mare all right?"

Belinda's response was, "So Jackson saved you? Wow, how romantic is that?"

Needing to work, Allie had shooed Belinda out of the barn and she and Megan had worked quietly for several hours before she'd glanced at her watch and realized something was wrong.

"The caterer," Allie said. "Did she happen to call?"

Megan shook her head. "No, why?"

"Her crew should have been here by now. I had no idea

it was so late." Allie could feel the panic growing. "And when I checked my date book…"

"What?" Megan asked.

"I wouldn't have canceled." But even as she was saying it, she was dialing the caterer's number.

A woman answered and Allie quickly asked about the dinner that was to be served at Cardwell Ranch tonight.

"We have you down for the reception in a few days, but… Wait a minute. It looks as if you did book it."

Allie felt relief wash through her, though it did nothing to relieve the panic. She had a ranch full of people to be fed and no caterer for the barbecue.

"I'm sorry. It says here that you called to cancel it yesterday."

"That's not possible. It couldn't have been me."

"Is your name Allie Taylor?"

She felt her heart drop. "Yes."

"It says here that you personally called."

Allie dropped into one of the chairs. She wanted to argue with the woman, but what good would it do? The damage was done. And anyway, she couldn't be sure she hadn't called. She couldn't be sure of anything.

"Just make sure that the caterers will be here on the Fourth of July for the wedding reception and that no one, and I mean not even me, can cancel it. Can you do that for me?" Her voice broke and she saw Megan looking at her with concern.

As she disconnected, she fought tears. "What am I going to do?"

"What's wrong?"

Her head snapped up at the sound of Jackson's voice. "I thought you were having beers with your brothers?"

"A couple beers is all I can handle. So come on, what's going on?"

She wiped at her eyes, standing to turn her back to him until she could gain control. What the man must think of her.

"The caterer accidentally got canceled. Looks like we might have to try to find a restaurant tonight," Megan said, reaching for her phone.

"Don't be ridiculous," Jackson said, turning Allie to look at him. "You have some of the best barbecue experts in the country right here on the ranch. I'll run down to the market and get some ribs while my brothers get the fire going. It's going to be fine."

This last statement Allie could tell was directed at her. She met his gaze, all her gratitude in that one look.

Jackson tipped his hat and gave her a smile. "It's going to be better than fine. You'll see."

"I HOPE YOU don't mind," Allie heard Jackson tell Dana and Lily. "I changed Allie's plans. I thought it would be fun if the Cardwell boys barbecued."

Dana was delighted and so was Lily. They insisted she, Natalie, Megan and Belinda stay and Allie soon found herself getting caught up in the revelry.

The Texas Boys Barbecue brothers went to work making dinner. Allie felt awful that they had to cook, but soon saw how much fun they were having.

They joked and played around while their father and Dana's provided the music. All the ranch hands and neighbors ended up being invited and pretty soon it had turned into a party. She noticed that even Drew, who'd been working at one of the cabins, had been invited to join them.

The barbecue was amazing and a lot more fun than the one Allie had originally planned. Everyone complimented the food and the new restaurant was toasted as a welcome addition to Big Sky.

Allie did her best to stay in the background. The day had left her feeling beaten up from her wild horseback ride to the foul-up with the caterer, along with her other misadventures. She was just happy to sit on the sidelines. Megan and Belinda were having a ball dancing with some of the ranch hands. All the kids were dancing, as well. At one point, she saw Jackson showing Ford how to do the swing with Natalie.

Someone stepped in front of her, blocking her view of the dance floor. She looked up to see Drew.

"I don't believe you've danced all night," he said.

"I'm really not—"

"What? You won't dance with your own brother-in-law? I guess you don't need me anymore now that you have the Cardwells. Or is it just one Cardwell?"

She realized he'd had too much to drink. "Drew, that isn't—"

"Excuse me," Jackson said, suddenly appearing beside her. "I believe this dance is mine." He reached for Allie's hand.

Drew started to argue, but Jackson didn't give him a chance before he pulled Allie out onto the dance floor. The song was a slow one. He took her in his arms and pulled her close.

"You really have to quit saving me," she said only half joking.

"Sorry, but I could see you needed help," Jackson said. "Your brother-in-law is more than a little protective, Allie."

She didn't want to talk about Drew. She closed her eyes for a moment. It felt good in the cowboy's arms. She couldn't remember the last time she'd danced, but that felt good, too, moving to the slow country song. "You saved my life earlier and then saved my bacon tonight. Natalie thinks you're a cowboy superhero. I'm beginning to wonder myself."

He gave her a grin and a shrug. "It weren't nothin', ma'am," he said, heavy on the Texas drawl. "Actually, I don't know why my brothers and I hadn't thought of it before. You did me a favor. I'd missed cooking with them. It was fun."

"Did I hear there is a bachelor party tomorrow night?"

Jackson groaned. "Hayes is in charge. I hate to think." He laughed softly. "Then the rehearsal and dinner the next night and finally the wedding." He shook his head as if he couldn't wait for it to be over.

Allie had felt the same way—before she'd met Jackson Cardwell.

Drew appeared just then. "Cuttin' in," he said, slurring his words as he pried himself between the two of them.

Jackson seemed to hesitate, but Allie didn't want trouble. She stepped into Drew's arms and let him dance her away from the Texas cowboy.

"What the hell do you think you're doing?" Drew demanded as he pulled her closer. "My brother is barely cold in his grave and here you are actin' like—"

"The wedding planner?" She broke away from him as the song ended. "Sorry, but I'm calling it a night. I have a lot of work to do tomorrow." With that she went to get Natalie. It was time to go home.

Chapter Six

Allie was getting ready to go to the ranch the next morning when she heard a vehicle pull up. She glanced out groaning when she saw it was Drew. Even more disturbing, he had his mother with him. As she watched them climb out, she braced herself for the worst. Drew had been acting strangely since he'd seen her with Jackson that first time.

"Hi," she said opening the door before either of them could knock. "You just caught me heading out."

"We *hoped* to catch you," Mildred said. "We're taking Natalie for the day so you can get some work done."

Not may we, but *we're taking.* "I'm sorry but Natalie already has plans."

Mildred's eyebrow shot up. "Natalie is five. Her plans can change."

"Natalie is going with the Cardwells—"

"The Cardwells aren't family," Mildred spat.

No, Allie thought, *but I wish they were.* "If you had just called—"

"I'm sure Nat would rather spend the day with her grandmother than whatever you have planned for—" Mildred broke off at the sound of a vehicle coming up the road toward them.

Who now? Allie wondered, fearing she was about to lose this battle with her in-laws—and break her daughter's heart. Her pulse did a little leap as she recognized the SUV as the one Jackson Cardwell had been driving yesterday. But what was he doing here? Allie had said she would bring Nat to the ranch.

Jackson parked and got out, Ford right behind him. He seemed to take in the scene before he asked, "Is there a problem?"

"Nothing to do with you," Drew said.

"Jackson Cardwell," he said and held out his hand. "I don't believe we've been formally introduced."

Drew was slow to take it. "Drew Taylor." Allie could see her brother-in-law sizing up Jackson. While they were both a few inches over six feet and both strong-looking, Jackson had the broader shoulders and looked as if he could take Drew in a fair fight.

Mildred crossed her arms over her chest and said, "We're here to pick up my granddaughter."

"That's why *I'm* here," Jackson said. Just then Natalie came to the door. She was dressed for the rodeo in her Western shirt, jeans and new red cowboy boots. Allie had braided her hair into two plaits that trailed down her back. A straw cowboy hat was perched on her head, her smile huge.

"I'm going to the rodeo with Ford and Hank and Mary," Nat announced excitedly. Oblivious to what was going on, she added, "I've never been to a rodeo before."

"Hop into the rig with Ford. I borrowed a carseat from Dana," Jackson said before either Drew or Mildred could argue otherwise.

With a wave, Nat hurried past her grandmother and uncle and taking Ford's hand, the two ran toward the SUV.

Allie held her breath as she saw Drew ball his hands into fists. She'd never seen him like this and realized Jackson was right. This was more than him being protective.

Jackson looked as if he expected Drew to take a swing— and was almost daring him to. The tension between the two men was thick as fresh-churned butter. Surely it wouldn't come to blows.

"Are you ready?" Jackson said to her, making her blink in surprise. "Dana gave me your ticket for the rodeo."

He *knew* she wasn't planning to go. This wedding had to be perfect and let's face it, she hadn't been herself for some time now.

"Going to a rodeo is part of this so-called wedding planning?" Mildred demanded. She lifted a brow. "I heard it also entails dancing with the guests."

"All in a day's work," Jackson said and met Allie's gaze. "We should get going. Don't want to be late." He looked to Drew. "Nice to meet you." Then turned to Mildred. "You must be Allie's mother-in-law."

"Mildred." Her lips were pursed so tightly that the word barely came out.

"I just need to grab my purse," Allie said, taking advantage of Jackson's rescue, even though she knew it would cost her.

When she came back out, Jackson was waiting for her. He tipped his hat to Drew and Mildred as Allie locked the cabin door behind her. She noticed that Mother Taylor and Drew were still standing where she'd left them, both looking infuriated.

She hated antagonizing them for fear what could happen if they ever decided to try to take Natalive from her. If they knew about just a few of the so-called incidents...

Like Nat, Allie slipped past them out to the SUV and didn't let out the breath she'd been holding until she was seated in the passenger seat.

"That looked like an ambush back there," Jackson said as they drove away.

She glanced back knowing she might have escaped this time, but there would be retribution. "They mean well."

JACKSON GLANCED OVER at her. "Do they?"

She looked away. "With Nick gone… Well, we're all adjusting to it. I'm sure they feel all they have left of him is Nat. They just want to see more of her."

He could see that she felt guilty. His ex and her family had used guilt on him like a club. He remembered that beat-up, rotten feeling and hated to see her going through it.

In the backseat, Natalie was telling Ford about something her horse had done yesterday during her ride. They both started laughing the way only kids can do. He loved the sound.

"Thank you for the rescue, but I really can't go to the rodeo. You can drop me at the ranch," Allie said, clearly nervous. "I need to check on things."

"You've done a great job. A few hours away at the rodeo is your reward. Dana's orders. She's the one who sent me to get you, knowing you wouldn't come unless I did."

"I really should be working."

"When was the last time you were at a rodeo?" he asked.

She chewed at her lower lip for a moment. "I think I went with some friends when I was in the fifth grade."

He smiled over at her. "Well, then it is high time you went again."

"I want an elephant ear!" Ford cried from the backseat.

"An elephant ear?" Nat repeated and began to giggle.

"So Nat's never been to a rodeo, either?" Jackson asked.

"No, I guess she hasn't."

"Well, she is going today and she and her mother are going to have elephant ears!" he announced. The kids laughed happily. He was glad to hear Ford explaining that an elephant ear really was just fried bread with sugar and cinnamon on it, but that it was really good.

Allie seemed to relax, but he saw her checking her side mirror. Did she think her in-laws would chase her down? He wouldn't have been surprised. They'd been more than overbearing. He had seen how they dominated Allie. It made him wonder what her husband had been like.

When they reached the rodeo grounds, Dana and Hud were waiting along with the kids and Tag and Lily and Hayes and McKenzie and Laramie.

"Oh, I'm so glad you decided to come along," Dana said when she saw Allie. "Jackson said he wasn't sure he could convince you, but he was darned sure going to try." She glanced at her cousin. "He must be pretty persuasive."

"Yes, he is," Allie said and smiled.

Jackson felt a little piece of his heart float up at that smile.

Easy, Texas cowboy, he warned himself.

But even as he thought it, he had to admit that he was getting into the habit of rescuing this woman—and enjoying it. Allie needed protecting. How badly she needed it, he didn't yet know.

It was the least he could do—until the wedding. And then he and Ford were headed back to Texas. Allie Taylor would be on her own.

Just the thought made him scared for her.

ALLIE COULDN'T REMEMBER the last time she'd had so much fun. The rodeo was thrilling, the elephant ear delicious and the Cardwells a very fun family. She'd ended up sitting next to Jackson, their children in front of them.

"I want to be a barrel racer," Natalie announced.

"We'll have to set up some barrels at the ranch," Dana said. "Natalie's a natural in the saddle. She'd make a great barrel racer."

"Well, I'm not riding the bulls," Ford said and everyone laughed.

"Glad you came along?" Jackson asked Allie as he offered some of his popcorn.

She'd already eaten a huge elephant ear and loved every

bite, but she still took a handful of popcorn and smiled. "I am. This is fun."

"You deserve some fun."

Allie wasn't so sure about that. She wasn't sure what she deserved, wasn't that the problem? She leaned back against the bleachers, breathing in the summer day and wishing this would never end.

But it did end and the crowd began to make their way to the parking lot in a swell of people. That's when she saw him.

Nick. He was moving through the crowd. She'd seen him because he was going in the wrong direction—in their direction. He wore a dark-colored baseball cap, his features lost in the shadow of the cap's bill. She got only a glimpse— Suddenly, he turned as if headed for the parking lot, as well. She sat up, telling herself her eyes were deceiving her. Nick was dead and yet—

"Allie, what it is?" Jackson asked.

In the past when she'd caught glimpses of him, she'd frozen, too shocked to move. She sprang to her feet and pushed her way down the grandstand steps until she reached the ground. Forcing her way through the crowd, she kept Nick in sight ahead of her. He was moving fast as if he wanted to get away.

Not this time, she thought, as she felt herself gaining on him. She could see the back of his head. He was wearing his MSU Bobcat navy ball cap, just like the one he'd been wearing the day he left to go up into the mountains—and his favorite shirt, the one she'd burned.

Her heart pounded harder against her ribs. She told herself she wasn't losing her mind. She couldn't explain any of this, but she knew what she was seeing. Nick. She was within yards of him, only a few people between them. She could almost reach out and grab his sleeve—

Suddenly, someone grabbed her arm, spinning her

around. She stumbled over backward, falling against the person in front of her, tripping on her own feet before hitting the ground. The fall knocked the air from her lungs and skinned her elbow, worse, her pride. The crowd opened a little around her as several people stopped to see if she was all right.

But it was Jackson who rushed to help her up. "Allie, are you all right?"

All she could do was shake her head as the man she thought was Nick disappeared into the crowd.

"WHAT'S GOING ON?" Jackson asked, seeing how upset she was. Had he said or done something that would make her take off like that?

She shook her head again as if unable to speak. He could tell *something* had happened. Drawing her aside, he asked her again. The kids had gone on ahead with Dana and her children.

"Allie, talk to me."

She looked up at him, those green eyes filling with tears. "I saw my husband, Nick. At least I think I saw him." She looked shocked as she darted a glance at the crowd, clearly expecting to see her dead husband again.

"You must think I'm crazy. *I* think I'm crazy. But I saw Nick. I know it couldn't be him, but it looked so much like him...." She shivered, even though the July day was hot. "He was wearing his new ball cap and his favorite shirt, the one I burned..." She began to cry.

"Hey," he said, taking her shoulders in his hands to turn her toward him. "I don't think you're crazy. I think you've had a horrible loss that—"

"I didn't *love* him. I was *leaving* him." The words tumbled out in a rush. "I...I...*hated* him. I *wanted* him gone, not dead!"

Jackson started to pull her into his arms, but she bolted

and was quickly swept up in the exiting crowd. He stood for a moment, letting her words sink in. Now, more than ever, he thought he understood why she was letting little things upset her. Guilt was a powerful thing. It explained a lot, especially with her relationship with her in-laws that he'd glimpsed that morning. How long had they been browbeating her? he wondered. Maybe her whole marriage.

He found himself more curious about her husband, Nick Taylor. And even more about Allie. Common sense told him to keep his distance. The wedding was only days away, then he and Ford would be flying back to Houston.

Maybe it was because he'd gone through a bad marriage, but he felt for her even more now. Like her, he was raising his child alone. Like her, he was disillusioned and he'd certainly gone through a time with his ex when he thought he was losing his mind. He'd also wished his ex dead more than once.

ALLIE CAUGHT UP to Dana as she was loading all the kids into her Suburban. Hud had brought his own rig since he had to stop by the marshal's office.

"Mind if I catch a ride with you?" Allie asked. "Jackson had some errands to run in town." The truth was that after her outburst, she was embarrassed and knew Dana had room for her and Nat in the Suburban.

"Of course not."

Allie had stopped long enough to go into the ladies' room and wash her face and calm down. She knew everyone had seen her take off like a crazy woman. She felt embarrassed and sick at heart, but mostly she was bone-deep scared.

When she'd seen Jackson heading for the parking lot, she'd motioned that she and Nat were going with Dana. He'd merely nodded, probably glad.

Dana didn't comment on Allie's red eyes or her impromptu exit earlier, though as she joined them at the Suburban. Instead, Dana made small talk about the rodeo, the weather, the upcoming wedding.

They were almost back to the ranch before Dana asked, "How are things going?" over the chatter of the kids in the back of the SUV.

Allie could tell that she wasn't just making conversation anymore. She really wanted to know. "It's been hard. I guess it's no secret that I've been struggling."

Dana reached over and squeezed her hand. "I know. I feel so bad about yesterday. I'm just so glad you weren't hurt." She smiled. "You did a great job of staying on that horse, though. I told Natalie how proud I was of you."

Allie thought of Jackson. He'd saved her life yesterday. She remembered the feel of his arms as he'd pulled her from the horse—and again on the dance floor last night. Shoving away the memory, she reminded herself that once the wedding was over, he and Ford would be leaving. She was going to have to start saving herself.

"Did Hud find out anything about who might have shot the horse?" she asked, remembering Hud talking to the vet when he'd stopped by to make sure the mare was all right.

"Nothing yet, but he is going to start gating the roads on the ranch. We can't keep people from the forest service property that borders the ranch, but we can keep them at a distance by closing off the ranch property. In the meantime, if there is anything I can do to help you…"

"Dana, you've already done so much. Letting Natalie come to the ranch and teaching her to ride…" Allie felt overwhelmed at Dana's generosity.

"Let's see if you thank me when she's constantly bugging you about buying her a horse," Dana joked. "Seriously, she can always come up to the ranch and ride. And if someday you do want a horse for her…"

"Thank you. For everything."

"I love what you've done to the barn," Dana said, changing the subject. "It is beyond my expectations and Lily can't say enough about it. I'm getting so excited, but then I'm a sucker for weddings."

"Me, too," Allie admitted. "They are so beautiful. There is so much hope and love in the air. It's all like a wonderful dream."

"Or fantasy," Dana joked. "Nothing about the wedding day is like marriage, especially four children later."

No, Allie thought, but then she'd had a small wedding in Mother Taylor's backyard. She should have known then how the marriage was going to go.

"Have you given any more thought to moving up to a guest cabin?" Dana asked.

"I have. Like I said, I'm touched by the offer. But Natalie has been through so many changes with Nick's death, I think staying at the cabin in her own bed might be best. We'll see, though. She is having such a great time at the ranch and as the wedding gets closer…"

"Just know that I saved a cabin for you and Natalie," Dana said. "And don't worry about your daughter. We have already adopted her into the family. The kids love her and Ford…." She laughed and lowered her voice, even though the kids weren't paying any attention behind them. "Have you noticed how tongue-tied he gets around her?"

They both laughed, Allie feeling blessed because she felt as if she, too, had been adopted into the family. The Cardwells were so different from the Taylors. She pushed that thought away. Just as she did the memory of that instant when she would have sworn she saw Nick at the rodeo.

Every time she thought she was getting better, stronger, something would happen to make her afraid she really was losing her mind.

"HEY," BELINDA SAID, seeming surprised when Allie and Nat walked into the barn that afternoon. "Where have you been? I thought you'd be here working."

"We went to the rodeo!" Natalie said. "And now I'm

going to go ride a horse!" With that she ran out of the barn to join the other kids and Dana.

"You went to the rodeo?"

"You sound like my in-laws," Allie said. "Yes, I was invited, I went and now I will do the last-minute arrangements for the rehearsal dinner tomorrow and it will all be fine."

Belinda lifted a brow. "Wow, what a change from the woman who was panicking because she couldn't find her keys the other day. Have you been drinking?"

"I'm taking my life back." She told her friend about the candle, Nick's shirt and what she did with it. Also about chasing the man she thought was Nick at the rodeo. "I almost caught him. If someone hadn't grabbed my arm…"

Belinda's eyes widened in alarm. "Sorry, but doesn't that sound a little…"

"Crazy? Believe me, I know. But I was sick of just taking it and doing nothing."

"I can see you thinking you saw someone who looked like Nick at the rodeo…."

"He was wearing his favorite shirt and his new ball cap."

Belinda stared at her. "The shirt you'd burned a few nights ago, right?"

Allie regretted telling her friend. "I know it doesn't make any sense. But all these things that have been happening? I'm not imagining them." From her friend's expression, she was glad she hadn't told her about the dresses or the new clothes she'd found in her closet.

"Sweetie," Belinda asked tentatively. "Did you give any more thought to making that call I suggested?"

"No and right now I have work to do."

"Don't we all. Some of us didn't spend the day at the rodeo."

Her friend actually sounded jealous. Allie put it out of her mind. She had to concentrate on the wedding. The barn looked beautiful. After the rehearsal dinner tomorrow night, she would get ready for the wedding. All she had to do was hold it together until then.

Megan came in with her list of last-minute things that needed to be tended to before the wedding rehearsal.

"I'll meet you down in the meadow in a few minutes." Left alone, Allie looked around the barn. She was a little sad it would be over. Jackson and Ford would be returning to Texas. Nat was really going to miss them.

And so are you.

ALLIE WASN'T SURE what awakened her. Dana had insisted she take the rest of the day off and spend it with Natalie.

"You have accomplished so much," Dana had argued. "Tomorrow is another day. The men are all going with Tag for his bachelor party tonight. I plan to turn in early with the kids. Trust me. We all need some downtime before the wedding."

Emotionally exhausted, Allie had agreed. She and Nat had come back to the cabin and gone down to the river until dinner. Nat loved building rock dams and playing in the water.

After dinner even Natalie was exhausted from the full day. After Allie had put her down to sleep, she'd turned in herself with a book. But only a few pages in, she had turned out the light and gone to sleep.

Now, startled awake, she lay listening to the wind that had come up during the night. It was groaning in the boughs of the pine trees next to the cabin. Through the window, she could see the pines swaying and smell the nearby river. She caught only glimpses of the moon in a sky filled with stars as she lay listening.

Since Nick's death she didn't sleep well. The cabin often woke her with its creaks and groans. Sometimes she would hear a thump as if something had fallen and yet when she'd gone to investigate, she would find nothing.

One time, she'd found the front door standing open. She had stared at it in shock, chilled by the cold air rushing in—and the knowledge that she distinctly remembered locking it before going to bed. Only a crazy woman would leave the front door wide open.

Now, though, all she heard was the wind in the pines, a pleasant sound, a safe sound. She tried to reassure herself that everything was fine. She thought of her day with the Cardwell family and remembered how Jackson had saved her by having the Cardwell brothers make their famous Texas barbecue for supper. She smiled at the memory of the brothers in their Texas Boys Barbecue aprons joking around as they cooked.

She'd overheard one of the brothers say he was glad to see Jackson loosening up a little. Allie found herself watching him earlier at the rodeo, wondering how he was doing as a single father. She didn't feel as if she'd done very well so far as a single mother.

Ford was having a sleepover at the main house at the ranch again tonight. Allie knew if Nat had known about it, she would have wanted to stay, as well. But she suspected that Dana had realized that she needed her daughter with her tonight. What a day! First a run-in earlier with Mildred and Drew... Allie felt a chill at the memory. They had both been so furious and no doubt hurt, as well. Then thinking she saw Nick. She shook her head and, closing her eyes, tried to will herself to go back to sleep. If she got to thinking about any of that—

A small thump made her freeze. She heard it again and quickly swung her legs over the side of the bed. The sound had come from down the hall toward the bedroom where Natalie was sleeping.

Allie didn't bother with her slippers or her robe; she was too anxious as she heard another thump. She snapped on the hall light as she rushed down the short, narrow hallway to her daughter's room. The door she'd left open was now closed. She stopped in front of it, her heart pounding. The wind. It must have blown it shut. But surely she hadn't left Nat's window open that much.

She grabbed the knob and turned, shoving the door open with a force that sent her stumbling into the small room. The moon and starlight poured in through the gaping open window to paint the bedroom in silver as the wind slammed a loose shutter against the side of the cabin with a thump.

Allie felt her eyes widen as a scream climbed her throat.

Nat's bed was empty.

Chapter Seven

Jackson felt at loose ends after the bachelor party. Part of the reason, he told himself, was because he'd spent so little time with his son. Back in Texas on their small ranch, he and Ford were inseparable. It was good to see his son having so much fun with other children, but he missed him.

Tonight Ford was having a sleepover at the main house with Dana's brood. He'd wanted to say no when Dana had asked, but he had seen that Ford had his heart set and Jackson had no choice but to attend Tag's bachelor party.

Fortunately, it had been a mild one, bar-hopping from the Corral to Lily's brother's bar at Big Sky, The Canyon Bar. They'd laughed and joked about their childhoods growing up in Texas and talked about Tag's upcoming wedding and bugged Hayes about his plans with McKenzie. Hayes only grinned in answer.

Hud, as designated driver, got them all home just after midnight, where they parted company and headed to their respective cabins. That was hours ago. Jackson had slept for a while before the wind had awakened him.

Now, alone with only his thoughts, he kept circling back to Allie. She'd had fun at the rodeo—until she'd thought she'd seen her dead husband. He blamed her in-laws. He figured they'd been laying a guilt trip on her ever since Nick Taylor had been presumed dead. Her run-in with them that morning must have made her think she saw Nick. He wanted to throttle them for the way they treated Allie and shuddered at the thought of them having anything to do with raising Natalie.

Allie was too nice. Did she really believe they meant well? Like hell, he thought now. They'd been in the wrong and yet they'd made her feel badly. It reminded him too much of the way his ex had done him.

It had been fun cooking with his brothers again—just as they had when they'd started their first barbecue restaurant. Allie'd had fun at the barbecue, too. He'd seen her laughing and smiling with the family. He'd enjoyed himself, as well. Of course Austin still hadn't arrived. But it was nice being with the others.

As much as he'd enjoyed the day, he felt too antsy to sleep and admitted it wasn't just Ford who was the problem. He tried to go back to sleep, but knew it was impossible. He had too much on his mind. Except for the wind in the pines, the ranch was quiet as he decided to go for a walk.

Overhead the Montana sky was a dazzling glitter of starlight with the moon peeking in and out of the clouds. The mountains rose on each side of the canyon, blacker than midnight. A breeze stirred the dark pines, sending a whisper through the night.

As he neared his rental SUV, he decided to go for a ride. He hadn't had that much to drink earlier and, after sleeping for a few hours, felt fine to drive.

But not far down the road, he found himself slowing as he neared Allie's cabin. The cabin was small and sat back from the highway on the river.

He would have driven on past, if a light hadn't come on inside the cabin.

Something about that light coming on in the wee hours of the morning sent a shiver through him. He would have said he had a premonition, if he believed in them. Instead, he didn't question what made him turn down her road.

Just as he pulled up to the cabin, Allie came running out.

At first he thought she'd seen him turn into her yard and that was why she'd come running out with a flashlight. But one look at her wild expression, her bare feet and her clothed in nothing but her nightgown, and he knew why he'd turned into her cabin.

"Allie?" he called to her as he jumped out. "Allie, what's wrong?"

She didn't seem to hear him. She ran toward the side of the cabin as if searching furiously as her flashlight beam darted into the darkness. He had to run after her as she headed around the back of the cabin. He grabbed her arm, thinking she might be having a nightmare and was walking in her sleep.

"Allie, what's wrong?"

"Nat! She's gone!"

He instantly thought of the fast-moving river not many yards out the back door. His gaze went to Allie's feet. "Get some shoes on. I'll check behind the house."

Taking her flashlight, he pushed her toward the front door before running around to the back of the cabin. He could hear and smell the river on the other side of a stand of pines. The July night was cool, almost cold this close to the river. Through the dark boughs, he caught glimpses of the Gallatin River. It shone in the moon and starlight, a ribbon of silver that had spent eons carving its way through the granite canyon walls.

As he reached the dense pines, his mind was racing. Had Natalie gotten up in the night and come outside? Maybe half-asleep, would she head for the river?

"Natalie!" he called. The only answer was the rush of the river and moan of the wind in the pine boughs overhead.

At the edge of the river, he shone the flashlight beam along the edge of the bank. No tracks in the soft earth. He flicked the light up and down the area between the pines, then out over the water. Exposed boulders shone in the light as the fast water rushed over and around them.

If Natalie had come down here and gone into the swift current…

At the sound of a vehicle engine starting up, he swung his flashlight beam in time to see a dark-colored pickup take off out of the pines. Had someone kidnapped Natalie? His first thought was the Taylors.

As he ran back toward the cabin, he tried to tell himself it had probably been teenagers parked down by the river making out. Once inside, he found Allie. She'd pulled on sandals and a robe and had just been heading out again. She looked panicked, her cheeks wet with tears.

"You're sure she isn't somewhere in the house," he said, thinking about a time that he'd fallen asleep under his bed while his mother had turned the house upside down looking for him.

The cabin was small. It took only a moment to search everywhere except Nat's room. As he neared the door to the child's bedroom, he felt the cool air and knew before he pushed open the door that her window was wide open, the wind billowing the curtains.

He could see the river and pines through the open window next to the bed. No screen. What looked like fresh soil and several dried pine needles were on the floor next to the bed. As he started to step into the room, a sound came from under the covers on the bed.

Jackson was at the bed in two long strides, pulling back the covers to find a sleeping Natalie Taylor curled there.

Had she been there the whole time and Allie had somehow missed her?

Allie stumbled into the room and fell to her knees next to her daughter's bed. She pulled Nat to her, snuggling her face into the sleeping child.

Jackson stepped out of the room to leave them alone for

a moment. His heart was still racing, his fear now for Allie rather than Nat.

A few minutes later, Allie came out of her daughter's room. He could see that she'd been crying again.

"She's such a sound sleeper. I called for her. I swear she wasn't in her bed."

"I believe you."

"I checked her room. I looked under her bed...." The tears began to fall again. "I looked in her closet. I called her name. *She wasn't there.* She wasn't anywhere in the cabin."

"It's all right," Jackson said as he stepped to her and put his arms around her.

Her voice broke as she tried to speak again. "What if she was there the whole time?" she whispered against his chest. He could feel her trembling and crying with both relief and this new fear. "She can sleep through anything. Maybe—"

"Did you leave the window open?"

"I cracked it just a little so she could get fresh air...."

"Natalie isn't strong enough to open that old window all the way like that."

Allie pulled back to look up at him, tears welling in her green eyes. "I *must* have opened it. I *must* have—"

He thought of the pickup he'd seen leaving. "There's something I need to check," he said, picking up the flashlight from where he'd laid it down just moments before. "Stay here with Natalie."

Outside he moved along the side of the house to the back, shining the flashlight ahead of him. He suspected what he would find so he wasn't all that surprised to discover the boot prints in the soft dirt outside Nat's window.

Jackson knelt down next to the prints. A man-size boot. He shone the light a few feet away. The tracks had come up to the window, the print a partial as if the man had sneaked up on the toes of his boots. But when the prints retreated from the child's window, the prints were full boot tracks, deep in the dirt as if he'd been carrying something. The tracks disappeared into the dried needles of the pines, then reappeared, this time headed back to the house. When the man had returned Natalie to her bed—and left dried pine needles and dirt on the bedroom floor.

ALLIE SAT ON the edge of her daughter's bed. She'd always loved watching Natalie sleep. There was something so incredibly sweet about her that was heightened when she slept. The sleep of angels, she thought as she watched the rise and fall of her daughter's chest.

Outside the now closed window, Jackson's shadow appeared and disappeared. A few minutes later, she heard him come back into the cabin. He came directly down the hall, stopping in Nat's bedroom doorway as if he knew she would be sitting on the side of the bed, watching her daughter sleep. That was where he would have been if it had been his son who'd gone missing, he thought.

She was still so shaken and scared. Not for Natalie, who was safe in her bed, but for herself. How could she have thought her daughter was missing? She really was losing her mind. Tucking Nat in, she checked to make sure the window was locked and left the room, propping the door open.

Jackson followed her into the small living room. She held her breath as she met his gaze. He was the one person who had made her feel as if she was going to be all right. He'd seen the black cat. He'd sympathized with her when she'd told him about misplacing her car keys and messing up her date book.

But earlier he'd looked at her as if she were a hysterical woman half out of her mind. She *had* been. Maybe she *was* unstable. When she'd found Nat's bed empty— Just the thought made her blood run cold again.

"I swear to you she wasn't in her bed." She could hear how close she was to breaking down again.

He must have, too, because he reached over and gripped her arm. "You didn't imagine it any more than you did the black cat."

She stared at him. "How can you say that?"

"Someone was outside Natalie's window tonight. There were fresh tracks where he'd stood. He took Natalie."

Her heart began to thunder in her ears. "Someone tried to…" She couldn't bring herself to say the words as she imagined a shadowed man taking her baby girl out through the window. "But why…?"

"He must have heard me coming and changed his mind," Jackson said.

"Changed his mind?" This all felt too surreal. First Nick's death then all the insane incidents, now someone had tried to take her child?

"Why don't you sit down," Jackson suggested.

She nodded and sank into the closest chair. He took one and pulled it next to hers.

"Is there someone who would want to take your daughter?" he asked.

Again she stared at him, unable to speak for a moment. "Why would anyone want to kidnap Natalie? I don't have any money."

He seemed to hesitate. "What about your husband's family?"

JACKSON SAW THAT he'd voiced her fear. He'd seen the way her in-laws had been just that morning. It wasn't much of a stretch that they would try to take Natalie. But through an open window in the middle of the night?

"They've made no secret that they want to see her more, but to steal her from her bed and scare me like this?"

Scare her. He saw her eyes widen in alarm and he took a guess. "There have been other instances when something happened that scared you?"

Her wide, green eyes filled with tears. "It was nothing. Probably just my imagination. I haven't been myself since…"

"Tell me about the incidents."

She swallowed and seemed to brace herself. "I found a squirrel in my cast-iron pot that has a lid."

"A live squirrel?"

"Half dead. I know it sounds crazy. How could a squirrel get under a heavy lid like that?"

"It couldn't. What else?"

She blinked as if stunned that he believed her, but it seemed to free her voice. "My husband used to buy me clothes I didn't like. I found them all cut up but I don't remember doing it. My brother-in-law took Nat and me out for dinner and when I got back they were lying on the bed and there were new clothes in the closet, eight hundred dollars' worth, like I would have bought if…"

"If you had bought them. Did you?"

She hesitated. "I don't think so but there was a check missing from my checkbook and when I took them back to the store, the clerks didn't remember who'd purchased them."

"No one was ever around when any of these things happened?"

She shook her head. "When I told my mother-in-law about the squirrel in the pot…she thought I was still taking the drugs the doctor gave me right after Nick's death. The drugs did make me see things that weren't there.…" Her words fell away as if she'd just then realized something. "Unless the things *had* been there."

Allie looked up at him, tears shimmering in her eyes. "Like the black cat.… I wasn't sure I'd even seen it until you…"

It broke his heart. For months after her husband's death, she'd been going through this with no one who believed her.

"I don't think you imagined any of these things that have been happening to you," he said, reaching for her hand. "I think someone wants you to *believe* you are losing your mind. What would happen if you were?"

She didn't hesitate an instant. "I would lose Natalie."

AS RELIEVED AS she was, Allie had trouble believing what he was saying. She got up and started to make a fire.

"Let me do that," Jackson said, taking a handful of kindling from her.

Allie moved restlessly around the room as he got the blaze going. "You think it's someone in Nick's family?"

"That would be my guess. It's clear they want Natalie, especially your mother-in-law. Would her son, Drew, help her?"

She shook her head. "Nick would do whatever his mother wanted. But Drew…" She didn't want to believe it, but he seemed to have turned against her lately. She felt sick at the thought that she might have been wrong about him all this time.

"You must think I'm such a fool."

"My mother said be careful what family you're marrying into. I didn't listen. I didn't even *know* the woman I was really marrying. But then she hid it well—until we were married."

"I know exactly what you're saying."

His chuckle held no humor. "I learned the hard way."

"So did I. I would have left Nick, if he hadn't disappeared…. I suppose you heard that he went hiking up in the mountains late last fall and was believed killed by a grizzly."

He nodded. "I'm sorry. You must have all kinds of conflicting emotions under the circumstances."

Allie let out a sigh. "You have no idea. Or maybe you do. My friend Belinda says my so-called incidents are brought on by my guilt. She's even suggested that I see a psychic to try to contact Nick on the other side to make the guilt go away."

He shook his head. "I think there is a very sane explanation that has nothing to do with guilt, and the last thing you need is some charlatan who'll only take your money."

She laughed. "That was exactly what I thought." She couldn't believe how much better she felt. She hadn't felt strong for so long. Fear had weakened her, but Jackson's words brought out some of the old Allie, that strong young woman who'd foolishly married Nick Taylor.

He hadn't broken her at first. It had taken a few years before she'd realized what he'd done to her. She no longer had her own ideas—if they didn't agree with his. He dressed her, told her what friends he liked and which ones he didn't.

He'd basically taken over her life, but always making it seem as if he were doing her a favor since he knew best. And she had loved him. At least at first so she'd gone along because she hadn't wanted to upset him. Nick could be scary when he was mad. She'd learned not to set him off.

When Nick had been nice, he'd been so sweet that she had been lulled into thinking that if she was just a little more accommodating he would be sweet all the time.

"Belinda thinks Nick knew that I was leaving him and went up in the mountains to…"

"Kill himself? What do you think?" Jackson asked.

"Nick did say he wanted to change and that he was sorry about the way he'd acted, but…"

"You didn't believe it?"

She shook her head. "The Nick I knew couldn't change even if he'd wanted to."

So why had Nick Taylor gone up into the mountains last fall and never come back? Jackson wondered.

The fact that his body hadn't been found made Jackson more than a little suspicious. If the man had purposely gone to the mountains intending to die and leave his wife and child alone, then he was a coward. If he set the whole thing up and was now trying to have his wife committed…

The timing bothered him. His stomach roiled with anger at the thought. "Is there any chance he knew of your plans?"

"I didn't think so. For months I'd been picking up any change he left lying around. I also had been skimping on groceries so I could save a little. He might have noticed." She looked away guiltily. "I also took money out of his wallet if he'd been drinking. I figured he wouldn't know how much he spent. He never said anything."

Jackson hoped this bastard was alive because he planned to punch him before the man went to prison for what he was doing to this woman. Not letting her have her own money was a sin in any marriage, no matter what some head-of-the household types said.

"I hate to even ask this, but is there any chance—"

"Nick is still alive?" She stood and paced around the room. "That would explain it, wouldn't it? Why I think I see him or why I smell his aftershave in the house, even though I threw out the bottle months ago. Why when I start feeling better, he shows up."

"Like at the rodeo?" Jackson asked, feeling his skin crawl at the thought of the bastard. "This only happens when there is no one else around who sees him, right?"

She nodded. "It all happens in a split second so I can't be sure. At the rodeo, though, I almost caught him. Just a few more yards…" Allie's eyes suddenly widened. "I remember now. Someone grabbed my arm and spun me around. That's why I fell."

"You think it was someone who didn't want you to catch him."

"Did you see anyone you recognized in the crowd before you found me?"

He thought for a moment. "I wasn't looking for anyone

but you, I'm sorry. Allie, all of this is classic gaslighting. Someone wants to unnerve you, to make you think you're imagining things, to make you doubt your own reality and ultimately make you doubt your own sanity."

She met his gaze. Her eyes filled with tears. "You think it's Nick?"

"I think it's a possibility. If he suspected you were going to leave him and take Natalie…he might have staged his death. He had the most to lose if you left him and with his body never being found…"

NICK ALIVE? ALLIE felt a chill move through her. Her husband had been a ghost, haunting her from his mountain grave for months. Now he had taken on an even more malevolent spirit.

She got up and threw another log on the fire. But not even the hot flames could chase away the icy cold that had filled her at the thought of Nick still alive. Not just alive but stalking her, trying to make her think she was crazy. Still, why—

"You think he's after Natalie," she said and frowned. "He's never cared that much about her. He wanted a son and when he didn't get one…"

"Believe me. I know what it's like to have a vindictive spouse who would do anything to hurt me—including taking a child she didn't really want."

"Oh, Jackson, I'm so sorry."

"If your husband is alive, you can bet he is behind all of this."

If Nick really was alive, then Drew would know. It would also explain why Drew was being so protective and acting jealous over Jackson.

Jackson stepped to her. "There is one thing you can count on. It's going to get worse. Nick will have to escalate his plan. He probably has a story already planned for when he comes stumbling out of the mountains after being attacked and having no memory for months. But that story won't hold up if it goes on much longer. I don't want to scare you, but if whoever is behind this can't drive you crazy, they might get desperate and decide the best way to get Natalie is to get rid of her mother for good."

She shuddered.

"Sorry," he said. "I know it seems like a leap…"

Jackson looked to the dark window before returning his gaze to her. "But if your husband is alive, then you have to assume he is watching your every move."

If Nick wasn't, then Drew was doing it for him, she realized. "You really think it's possible?" she asked in a whisper as if not only was he watching but he was listening, as well.

"Given what has been happening to you and the fact that his body was never found?" Jackson nodded. "But if he is alive, we can't let him know that we're on to him."

We. That had such a wonderful sound. She had felt so alone in all this. Suddenly, she wasn't. Jackson believed her. He didn't think she was crazy. Far from it. He thought all of this was happening because someone wanted her to *believe* she was crazy. Maybe not just *someone,* but the man she'd married.

She swallowed back the bile that rose in her throat at the thought of how far her husband had gone and to what end? "He must have known I was leaving him and taking Natalie."

"That would be my guess. With you in the nuthouse, he could reappear and take your daughter."

The thought of Natalie with a man who would do something like that turned her blood to ice.

"But if he is alive, then—" Jackson seemed to hesitate "—then I really can't see how he could have pulled this off without help."

Allie knew what he was saying. Not just Drew but Mildred and Sarah might be in on this. "His brother, Drew, has been around a lot since Nick…disappeared and has helped out financially until the investigation is over. His mother's never liked me and didn't believe me when I've told her about only some of the things that have been happening. Or at least she pretended not to."

Jackson nodded. "What about Drew's sister, Sarah?"

"She's afraid of Mother Taylor, not that I can blame her."

He looked away for a moment. "What about the two women working with you on the wedding?"

"*Belinda and Megan?* Belinda's the only friend who stuck with me after I married Nick. He tried to run her off but she wasn't having any of it." Allie didn't want to believe it. Refused to. She shook her head. "She's been on my side against them. And Megan? She's my *stepsister* I never knew until…"

"Until?" he prompted.

"I guess it was right before Nick died. Megan contacted me. She was just finishing up her college degree at the University of Montana in Missoula. After my mother died, my father remarried several times and had more children. He moved away and I lost track of him and my step-siblings. Megan was like a gift coming into our lives when she did. Nat adores her. I adore her. You can't think she is somehow involved in any of this."

Jackson didn't say anything. He didn't have to. His skepticism was written all over his face. "It's the timing that bothers me."

She nodded. He thought she was naive. She'd always been too trusting. Isn't that what Nick had told her time and time again?

Allie quickly turned away as she felt hot tears scald her eyes. All of this was just too much. She thought of her daughter and hurriedly wiped at her tears. Straightening her back, she felt a surge of anger and turned back to face Jackson.

"Whoever is doing this, they aren't going to win. What do we do?" she asked.

"We catch them. Do you have a photograph of Nick?"

As she left the room, she noticed that the sun had come up. She came back with a snapshot. "This is the only one I could find. It's one of Nick and his brother, Drew. Nick is the one on the right."

Jackson looked down at the photo. "They look alike."

"Do they?" she said, looking at the snapshot he was holding. "I guess they do a little," she said, surprised that she hadn't noticed it because their personalities were so different. "Drew was always the quiet one. Nick was his mother's favorite. I'm sure that had something to do with why he was so cocky and smart-mouthed. Drew was the one always standing back watching."

"Did Drew resent that?" Jackson asked.

Allie frowned. "I don't know. He didn't seem to. Just the other day he was telling me how hard it was to keep the business going without Nick."

Jackson turned thoughtful for a moment. "You mentioned something about Belinda wanting you to see some psychic so you could reach Nick on the other side? I think you should do it."

Allie blinked in surprise. "Seriously? You don't think I'm messed up enough?"

"It's Belinda's idea, right? If she is involved, then this séance with the psychic is a trap. But since we are on to them now, it would help to know what they have planned for you. I suspect it won't be pleasant, though. I'm sure it is supposed to push you over the edge, if you aren't already dangling there. Do you think you can handle it?"

She raised her chin, her eyes dry, resolve burning in her like a blazing fire. She thought of the people who had been tricking her for months. Anger boiled up inside her along with a steely determination. She hadn't felt this strong in years. "I can handle it."

Jackson smiled at her. "Good." He checked his watch. "Give the psychic a call. Calling this early she will think you are desperate to see her, exactly what we want her to think."

Allie dug the card out, glad now that she'd saved it. She took a breath, let it out and dialed the number. Jackson stepped closer so he could hear.

She was surprised when a young-sounding woman answered after three rings.

"I'm sorry to call so early but I need your help. My friend Belinda suggested I call you." Jackson gave her a thumbs-up.

"You must be Allie. I was hoping you'd call. You're in danger—and so is your daughter. I need to see you as soon as possible."

"Is today too soon, then?" Allie asked.

"Why don't you come this evening, say about eight? Will that work for you?"

Allie met Jackson's gaze. He nodded. "That would be fine. I hope you can help me."

"I will do my best but ultimately it will be up to the spirits."

Jackson swore softly as Allie disconnected. "Spirits my ass. Between now and then, I will try to find out everything I can about the people with access to you." He reached over and took her hand. "Don't worry. We're going to catch these bastards."

Chapter Eight

When Jackson returned to the ranch, he found his brothers, told them what he thought was going on and asked for their help. He no longer kidded himself that he wasn't involved.

"I can talk to the cops about what they found in the mountains," Hayes said. "You say Nick Taylor's body still hasn't been found? Isn't that odd? He died late last fall and even with hikers in the area, no remains have turned up?"

"No, that's what makes me suspicious," Jackson said. "His claw-shredded backpack and rifle were discovered at the scene with grizzly prints in the dirt and enough blood to make them believe he was killed there. But still no remains of any kind."

Hayes nodded. "I'll get right on it."

"What can I do?" Laramie asked.

"Financials on everyone involved including Allie's friend Belinda Andrews and her stepsister, Megan Knight, as well as all of the Taylor family. Nick and his brother, Drew, were partners in a construction company called Gallatin Canyon Specialty Construction."

"You got it," Laramie said. "What about Allie herself?"

"Sure, and Nick, just in case he had something going on that she didn't know about," Jackson said.

"Wait a minute," Tag said. "What about me?"

"You, brother dear, are getting married. You just concentrate on your lovely bride-to-be," Jackson told him. Tag started to object. "If you're going to be hanging around the ranch here, then do me a favor. Keep an eye on Drew Taylor. He's apparently doing some repairs here."

Jackson stopped by the barn to find Allie and Megan hard at work putting together centerpieces for the tables. Allie pretended she needed something from her van and got up to go outside with him.

"No more trouble last night?" he asked, seeing worry in her gaze.

"None. I'm just having a hard time believing any of that happened last night." She glanced around as if she expected Nick to materialize before her gaze came back to him. Or maybe she was worried about her brother-in-law, Drew, seeing them together again. "I can't believe Belinda or Megan—"

"Have you seen Belinda?"

"She had to go into Bozeman. She left about twenty minutes ago, why?"

He shook his head. "You better get back inside. Try not to let on that you're suspicious."

She sighed. "You don't know how hard that is."

"I can imagine." He gave her an encouraging smile. "Just be your usual sweet self." He loved it when she returned his smile and those gorgeous dimples of hers showed.

As she went back into the barn and rejoined Megan, he headed up the hillside. Belinda was staying in the last guesthouse to the east. Each cabin was set away from the others in the dense pines for the most privacy.

A cool pine-scented breeze restlessly moved the boughs over his head as he walked on the bed of dried needles toward Belinda's cabin. He could hear the roar of the river and occasionally the sound of a semi shifting down on the highway far below. A squirrel chattered at him as he passed, breaking the tranquility.

He was almost to her cabin when he heard the crack of a twig behind him and spun around in surprise.

His brother Hayes grinned. "I would imagine the cabin will be locked," he said as he stepped on past to climb the steps to the small porch and try the door. "Yep, I know your lock-picking skills are rusty at best." He pulled out his tool set.

Jackson climbed the steps and elbowed his brother out of the way. "I told Dana I was locked out. She gave me the master key." He laughed and opened the door.

"You know I do this for a living, right?" his brother asked.

"I'd heard that. But are you any good?"

Hayes shot him a grin and headed for the log dresser in the room with the unmade bed.

Jackson glanced around the main room of the cabin and spotted Belinda's camera bag. He could hear his brother searching the bedroom as he carefully unzipped the bag. There were the usual items found in a professional photographer's large bag. He carefully took out the camera, lens and plastic filter containers and was about to put everything back, thinking there was nothing to find when he saw the corner of a photo protruding from one of the lower pockets.

"What did you find?" Hayes asked as he returned after searching both bedrooms.

Jackson drew out the photos and thumbed through them. They were shots taken with apparent friends. Each photo had Belinda smiling at the camera with her arm around different friends, all women. He was thinking how there wasn't one of her and Allie, when he came to the last photo and caught his breath.

"Who is that?" Hayes asked.

"Allie's husband, Nick, and her best friend Belinda Andrews. Allie said that Nick never liked Belinda." The snapshot had been taken in the woods along a trail. There was a sign in the distance that said Grouse Creek Trail. Nick had his arm possessively around Belinda. Both were smiling at each other rather than the camera the way lovers do.

"Apparently, they liked each other a lot more than Allie knew," Hayes said. "But you know what is really interesting about that photo? That trailhead sign behind them."

"Let me guess. Up that trail is where Nick Taylor was believed to have been killed."

WHEN THEY'D FINISHED the centerpieces, Allie sent Megan into Bozeman for an order of wedding items that had been delayed. It had been difficult working with her and suspecting her of horrible things. Allie was relieved when she was finally alone in the barn.

Everything was coming along on schedule. It had been Dana's idea to start days early. "I don't want you to feel any pressure and if you need extra help, you just let me know," Dana had said.

"No, I'm sure that will be fine."

"I want you to have some free time to go for a horseback ride or just spend it on the ranch with your daughter."

"You are so thoughtful," Allie had said.

"Not at all. I just know what it's like with a little one, even though Natalie isn't so little anymore," she said with a laugh. "I promise I will keep your daughter busy so you can work and not have to worry about her having a good time."

Dana had been good to her word. Allie stepped outside the barn now to check on Natalie only to find her on the back of a horse about to take a short ride up the road for another picnic with Dana and the other children.

"Come along," Dana encouraged. "Warren would be happy to saddle you a horse. You know what they say about almost falling off a horse, don't you?" she asked with a smile. "You have to get back on."

Allie laughed, thinking that was exactly what she was

doing with her life, thanks to Jackson. She was tempted
to go on the ride until she saw him headed her way. "Next
time."

"We're going to hold you to it," Dana said. "In fact, we're
all going on a ride tomorrow before the rehearsal dinner.
Plan on coming along." With that they rode off, the kids
waving and cheering as they disappeared into the pines.

Jackson waved to his son, making the same promise before he continued on down the mountainside toward her.

When she saw his expression, her heart fell. He'd discovered something and whatever it was, it wasn't good.

"Let's go up to my cabin," Jackson said as he glanced
around. "We can talk there."

They made the short hike up the mountainside. His cabin
faced the river, sheltered in the pines and was several dozen
yards from the closest cabin where his brothers were staying together.

"What is it?" Allie asked the moment they were inside.

Jackson handed her a snapshot in answer.

She looked down at her smiling husband and her best
friend. There was no doubt what she was looking at but still
she was shocked and found it hard to believe. For more than
six years Belinda and Nick had acted as if they couldn't
stand each other. Had it been a lie the entire time?

"When was this taken?" she asked.

Jackson shook his head. "There isn't a date. I found it
in her camera bag with a lot of other photos of her with
friends."

Allie raised an eyebrow. "You aren't going to try to convince me that they are just friends."

He shook his head. "You weren't at all suspicious?"

She laughed as she made her way to the couch and sat
down. The ground under her feet no longer felt stable. "Nick
always said I was too trusting. Belinda was the only friend

who could put up with Nick. So I guess a part of me suspected that Nick liked her more than he let on."

"I'm sorry."

"Don't be. I stopped loving Nick Taylor the year we got married. If I hadn't gotten pregnant with Nat…" She tossed the photo on the coffee table in front of her.

"She was the only one you told about your plans to leave Nick?" he asked as he took a seat across from her.

Allie let out a laugh. "So of course she told him."

"More than likely," he agreed. "There's more." He took a breath and let it out as he studied her. "You sure you want to hear all of this?"

She sat up straighter. "Let me have it."

"I got my brothers to help me. They have the expertise in their chosen fields that we needed. Hayes talked to the cops who had a copy of Nick's file with reports from the hiker who found the backpack and rifle to the warden who investigated the initial scene. He reported that there was sufficient evidence to assume that Nick was dead based on the shredded backpack and the amount of blood soaked into the pine needles."

"So…he's dead?"

"Or he made it look that way," Jackson said. "No DNA was tested at the scene because there didn't appear to be a need to do so. But there are still a lot of questions. No shots were fired from the rifle, leading the investigators to believe he didn't have time to get off a shot before he was attacked by the bear. Or he could have staged the whole thing. But the incidents you've been having with things disappearing and reappearing, those can't be Nick. If he's alive, he has to keep his head down."

"So we're back to my in-laws and Belinda and Megan."

"I'm afraid so. Belinda, if involved with Nick, would be the obvious one. Was she around before any of the incidents happened?"

FREE Merchandise is 'in the Cards' for you!

Dear Reader,

We're giving away FREE MERCHANDISE!

Seriously, we'd like to reward you for reading this novel by giving you **FREE MERCHANDISE** worth over **$20**. And no purchase is necessary!

You see the Jack of Hearts sticker above? Paste that sticker in the box on the Free Merchandise Voucher inside. Return the Voucher promptly...and we'll send you valuable Free Merchandise!

Thanks again for reading one of our novels—and enjoy your Free Merchandise with our compliments!

Pam Powers

Pam Powers

P.S. Look inside to see what Free Merchandise is **"in the cards"** for you!

W e'd like to send you two free books like the one you are enjoying now. Your two books have a combined price of over $10, but they are yours to keep absolutely FREE! We'll even send you 2 wonderful surprise gifts. You can't lose!

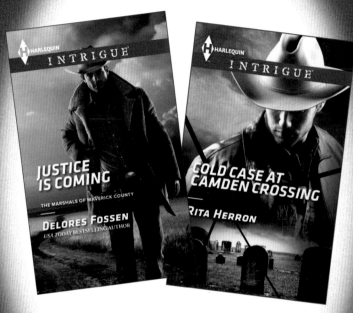

REMEMBER: Your Free Merchandise, consisting of **2 Free Books** and **2 Free Gifts**, is worth over $20.00! No purchase is necessary, so please send for your Free Merchandise today.

Get TWO FREE GIFTS!
We'll also send you two wonderful FREE GIFTS (worth about $10), in addition to your 2 Free books!

Visit us at:
www.ReaderService.com

YOUR FREE MERCHANDISE INCLUDES...

2 FREE Books **AND** 2 FREE Mystery Gifts

FREE MERCHANDISE VOUCHER

2 FREE BOOKS and **2 FREE GIFTS**

Please send my Free Merchandise, consisting of
2 Free Books and **2 Free Mystery Gifts**.
I understand that I am under no obligation to buy
anything, as explained on the back of this card.

❏ I prefer the regular-print edition
182/382 HDL GEZN

❏ I prefer the larger-print edition
199/399 HDL GEZN

Please Print

FIRST NAME

LAST NAME

ADDRESS

APT.#   CITY

STATE/PROV.   ZIP/POSTAL CODE

Offer limited to one per household and not applicable to series that subscriber is currently receiving.
Your Privacy—The Harlequin® Reader Service is committed to protecting your privacy. Our Privacy Policy is available online at www.ReaderService.com or upon request from the Harlequin Reader Service. We make a portion of our mailing list available to reputable third parties that offer products we believe may interest you. If you prefer that we not exchange your name with third parties, or if you wish to clarify or modify your communication preferences, please visit us at www.ReaderService.com/consumerschoice or write to us at Harlequin Reader Service Preference Service, P.O. Box 9062, Buffalo, NY 14269. Include your complete name and address.

NO PURCHASE NECESSARY!

HI-714-FM13

► Detach card and mail today. No stamp needed. ►

© 2013 HARLEQUIN ENTERPRISES LIMITED. ® and ™ are trademarks owned and used by the trademark owner and/or its licensee. Printed in the U.S.A.

Allie thought back to when her keys had ended up in the bathroom sink at the Mexican restaurant. She'd left her purse at the table, but then Sarah and her mother had been there, too. She sighed, still refusing to believe it, even after seeing the photo. "Yes, but Belinda wouldn't—"

"Wouldn't have an affair with your husband behind your back?"

"She's been so *worried* about me."

Jackson raised a brow.

Allie hugged herself against the thought of what he was saying. Belinda *had* apparently betrayed her with Nick. Maybe Jackson was right. Then she remembered something. "Belinda has a new man in her life. I know the signs. She starts dressing up and, I don't know, acting different. The man can't be Nick. That photo doesn't look recent of her and Nick. Why would she be acting as if there was someone new if it was Nick all these months?"

"Maybe he's been hiding out and has only now returned to the canyon."

That thought turned her stomach. "If he's come back…"

"Then whoever has been gaslighting you must be planning on stepping up their plan," Jackson said.

She turned to look at him as a shiver raced through her. "The psychic. Maybe this is their grand finale, so to speak, and they have something big planned tonight to finally send me to the loony bin."

"Maybe you shouldn't go—"

"No. Whatever they have planned, it won't work. They've done their best to drive me crazy. I know now what they're up to. I'll be fine."

"I sure hope so," Jackson said.

"WHAT IS THE lowdown on the Taylor family?" Jackson asked Hud after dinner that evening at the ranch. They'd had beef steaks cooked on a pitchfork in the fire and eaten on the wide porch at the front of the house. The night had been beautiful, but Jackson was too antsy to appreciate it. He was worried about Allie.

She'd dropped Natalie by before she and Belinda had left. He hadn't had a chance to speak with her without raising suspicion. All he could do was try his best to find out who was behind the things that had been happening to her.

"Old canyon family," Hud said. "Questionable how they made their money. It was rumored that the patriarch killed someone and stole his gold." Hud shrugged. "Mildred? She married into it just months before Bud Taylor died in a car accident. She's kept the name even though she's been through several more husbands. I believe she is on number four now. Didn't take his name, though. He's fifteen, twenty years older and spends most of his time with his grown children back in Chicago."

"And the daughter?"

"Sarah?" Hud frowned. "Never been married that I know of. Lives in the guesthouse behind her mother's. No visible means of support."

"The brothers had a construction company together?"

"They did. Nick was the driving force. With him gone, I don't think Drew is working all that much."

"Just between you and me, Allie was planning to leave Nick Taylor before he went up in the mountain and disappeared," Jackson said, taking the marshal into his confidence.

Hud looked over at him. "What are you getting at?"

"Is there any chance Nick Taylor is alive?"

Hud frowned. "You must have some reason to believe he is."

"Someone has been gaslighting Allie."

"For what purpose?"

"I think someone, probably in the Taylor family, wants to take Natalie away from her."

"YOU SEEM BETTER," Belinda noted on the drive out of the canyon. She'd insisted on driving Allie to the psychic's house, saying she didn't trust Allie to drive herself if the psychic said anything that upset her.

Allie had been quiet most of the drive. "*Do* I seem better?" Did her friend seem disappointed in that?

"Maybe this isn't necessary."

That surprised her. "I thought you were the one who said I had to talk to this psychic?"

"I thought it would help."

"And now?" Allie asked.

"I don't want her to upset you when you seem to be doing so well."

"That's sweet, but I'm committed…so to speak."

Belinda nodded and kept driving. "Seriously, you seem so different and the only thing that has changed that I can tell is Jackson Cardwell showing up."

Allie laughed. "Just like you to think it has to be a man. Maybe I'm just getting control of my life."

Her friend looked skeptical. "Only a few days ago you were burning Nick's favorite shirt so it didn't turn up again."

"Didn't I tell you? The shirt *did* turn up again. I found it hanging in the shower this morning. Now I ask you, how is that possible?"

"You're sure you burned it? Maybe you just—"

"Dreamed it?" Allie smiled. That was what they wanted her to think. She looked over at Belinda, worried her old friend was up to her neck in this, whatever it was.

Allie fought the urge to confront her and demand to know who else was behind it. But Belinda turned down a narrow road, slowing to a stop in front of a small house with a faint porch light on.

Showtime, Allie thought as she tried to swallow the lump in her throat.

Chapter Nine

Belinda's apartment house was an old, five-story brick one a few blocks off Main Street in Bozeman.

Laramie waited in the car as lookout while Jackson and Hayes went inside. There was no password entry required. They simply walked in through the front door and took the elevator up to the third floor to room 3B. It was just as Allie had described it, an apartment at the back, the door recessed so even if someone had been home on the floor of four apartments, they wouldn't have seen Hayes pick the lock.

"You're fast," Jackson said, impressed.

Hayes merely smiled and handed him a pair of latex gloves. "I'm also smart. If you're right and Nick Taylor is alive and this becomes a criminal case… You get the idea. It was different up on the ranch. This, my brother, is breaking and entering."

Jackson pulled on the gloves and opened the door. As he started to draw his flashlight out of his pocket, Hayes snapped on an overhead light.

"What the—"

"Jackson," his brother said and motioned toward the window. The curtains were open, the apartment looking out onto another apartment building. While most of the curtains were drawn in those facing this way, several were open.

Hayes stepped to the window and closed the curtains.

"Nothing more suspicious than two dudes sneaking around in a woman's apartment with flashlights."

He had a point. "Let's make this quick."

"I'm with you," Hayes said and suggested the best place to start.

"If I didn't know better, I'd think you'd done this before," Jackson joked.

Hayes didn't answer.

In the bedroom in the bottom drawer of the bureau under a bunch of sweaters, Jackson found more photos of Belinda and Nick, but left them where he'd found them.

"So you think I'm right and Nick is alive," Jackson said.

Hayes shrugged.

Jackson finished the search of the bedroom, following his brother's instructions to try to leave everything as he had found it.

"Find anything?" he asked Hayes when he'd finished.

"She recently came into thirty-eight thousand dollars," Hayes said, thumbing through a stack of bank statements he'd taken from a drawer.

"Maybe it's a trust fund or an inheritance."

"Maybe. Or blackmail money or money Nick had hidden from Allie," Hayes said as he put everything back. "Laramie would probably be able to find out what it was if we had more time. Did you put the photos back?"

"All except one. I want to show it to Allie. It looks more recent to me."

Hayes looked as if he thought that was a bad idea. "You're messing with evidence," he reminded him.

"I'll take that chance," Jackson said.

His brother shook his head as he turned out the light and moved to the window to open the curtains like he'd found them.

"Does anyone else know how involved you are with the wedding planner?" Silence. "I didn't think so. Better not let cousin Dana find out or there will be hell to pay. She is very protective of people she cares about. She cares about that woman and her child. If you—"

"I'm not going to hurt her." He couldn't see his brother's expression in the dark. He didn't have to.

ALLIE BRACED HERSELF. She hadn't shared her fears about the visit with the psychic with Jackson before she'd left. She hadn't had to. She'd seen the expression on his face as he watched her leave. He was terrified for her.

For months someone had been trying to push her over the edge of sanity. She had a bad feeling that the psychic was part of the master plan, a shocker that was aimed at driving her insane. By now, they probably thought she was hanging on by a thread. While she was stronger, thanks to Jackson and his determination that she was perfectly sane and those around her were the problem, there was a part of her that wasn't so sure about that.

Just this morning, she'd stepped into the bathroom, opened the shower curtain and let out a cry of shock and disbelief. Nick's favorite shirt was hanging there, the same shirt she'd burned in the fireplace a few nights ago. Or at least one exactly like it. Worse, she smelled his aftershave and when she opened the medicine cabinet, there it was in the spot where he always kept it—right next to his razor, both of which she had thrown out months ago.

Had he hoped she would cut her wrists? Because it had crossed her mind. If it hadn't been for Natalie…and now Jackson…

"Remember, you're that strong woman you were before you met Nick Taylor," Jackson had said earlier.

She'd smiled because she could only vaguely remember that woman. But she wanted desperately to reacquaint herself with her. Now all she could do was be strong for her daughter. She couldn't let these people get their hands on Natalie.

Belinda parked in front of a small house and looked over at her. "Ready?"

Allie could hear reluctance in her friend's voice. If Jackson was right and Nick was behind this, then Allie suspected he was forcing Belinda to go through with the plan no matter what.

But that's what she had to find out. If Nick was alive. She opened her car door and climbed out. The night air was cool and scented with fresh-cut hay from a nearby field. It struck her how remote this house was. The closest other residence had been up the road a good half mile.

If a person was to scream, no one would hear, Allie thought, then warned herself not to bother screaming. Belinda and the psychic were probably hoping for just such a reaction.

"I was surprised when you agreed to do this," Belinda said now, studying her as she joined Allie on the path to the house.

"I told you. I would do anything to make whatever is happening to me stop." Allie took a deep breath and let it out. "Let's get this over with."

They walked up the short sidewalk and Belinda knocked. Allie noticed that there weren't any other vehicles around except for an old station wagon parked in the open, equally old garage. If Nick was here he'd either been dropped off or he'd parked in the trees at the back of the property.

The door was opened by a small, unintimidating woman wearing a tie-dyed T-shirt and worn jeans. Her feet were bare. Allie had been expecting a woman in a bright caftan wearing some sort of headdress. She was a little disappointed.

"Please come in," the woman said in what sounded like a European accent. "I am Katrina," she said with a slight nod. "It is so nice to meet you, Allie. Please follow me. Your friend can stay here."

Belinda moved to a couch in what Allie assumed was the sparsely furnished living area.

Allie followed the woman down a dim hallway and through a door into a small room dominated by a table and two chairs. The table was bare.

Katrina closed the door, making the room feel even smaller. She took a seat behind the desk and motioned Allie into the chair on the opposite side.

This felt silly and it was all Allie could do not to laugh. She and a friend in the fifth grade had stopped at the fortune teller's booth at the fair one time—her friend Willow's idea, not hers.

"I want to know if I am going to marry Curt," her friend had said.

Allie could have told her that there was a good chance she wasn't going to marry some boy in her fifth grade class.

The fortune teller had told them they would have long, happy lives and marry their true loves. Five dollars each later they were standing outside the woman's booth. Willow had been so excited, believing what the fortune teller had said was that she would marry Curt. She'd clearly read what she wanted into the woman's words.

Willow didn't marry Curt but maybe she had found her true love since she'd moved away in sixth grade when her father was transferred. Allie hadn't had a happy life nor had she apparently married her true love and now here she was again sitting across from some woman who she feared really might know her future because she was about to control it.

"I understand you want me to try to reach your husband who has passed over," Katrina said. "I have to warn you that I am not always able to reach the other side, but I will try since your friend seems to think if I can reach…"

"Nick," Allie supplied.

"Yes, that it will give you some peace." The woman hesitated. "I hope that will be the case. It isn't always, I must warn you. Do you want to continue?"

Allie swallowed and nodded.

"Give me your hands. I need you to think of your husband." Katrina dimmed the lights and reached across the table to take Allie's hands in hers. "It helps if you will close your eyes and try to envision your husband."

That was about the last thing Allie wanted to do, but as Katrina closed hers, Allie did the same. She couldn't help but think of Nick and wonder if he was watching her at this very moment.

WHILE WE'RE BREAKING the law, there is one other place I'd like to have a look before we head back," Jackson said to his brothers.

Hayes looked disapproving. "What part of breaking and entering don't you understand?"

"You can wait in the car."

Gallatin Canyon Specialty Construction was located on the outskirts of town next to a gravel pit. The industrial area was dark this time of the night as Jackson pulled in with his lights out and parked.

"Allie said the company hasn't been doing very well without Nick and wasn't doing that well even before Nick allegedly died," Jackson said. "I just want to take a look at the books."

"Good thing you brought me along," Laramie said. "You did mean, you want me to take a look, right?"

Jackson laughed. "Yeah, if you don't mind."

Hayes sighed and they all got out and walked toward the trailer that served as the office. Hayes unlocked the door then said, "I'll stand guard. Make it quick," before disappearing into the darkness.

"You do realize you might be jeopardizing everything by doing this," Laramie said. "Is this woman worth it?"

Jackson didn't answer as he pulled on the latex gloves Hayes had shoved at him in the car and handed his brother a pair before turning on a light and pointing at the file cabinets.

It wasn't until they were all three back in the car and headed south toward Cardwell Ranch that Jackson asked his brother what he'd found, if anything.

After Laramie tried to explain it in fiduciary terms, Hayes snapped, "The bottom line, please."

Laramie sighed. "It is clear why you all leave the business part of Texas Boys Barbecue up to me. All right, here it is. Drew Taylor is broke and has been siphoning off the money from the business before the sale."

"Sale?" Jackson said.

"While not of general knowledge, Drew has been trying to sell the business through a company in other states."

"That's suspicious," Hayes said.

"Is his mother involved in the construction business?" Jackson asked.

Laramie chuckled. "Excellent question. I believe she might have been a silent partner, which I take to mean she provided some of the money. Until recently, Drew was writing her a check each month."

"Think she knows what her son is up to?" Hayes asked.

"Doubtful. According to Allie, Mother Taylor rules the roost. Everyone is afraid of her."

"Sounds like our boy Drew is planning to escape in the dark of night," Hayes commented and Jackson agreed.

"As for the rest of the people you asked me to look at the finances of, Mildred Taylor is fine as long as her old, absentee husband sends her a check each month. She and her daughter live off the old man. Nick wasn't much of a breadwinner. Montana winters slow down construction, apparently. But he did okay. After his death, there wasn't much in his personal account."

"So the thirty-eight thousand Belinda just received wasn't from Nick, then," Hayes said.

Laramie continued, "Nick did, however, leave a hundred-thousand-dollar insurance policy, which is supposed to pay out any day once Nick has finally been ruled legally deceased."

"A hundred thousand?" Jackson exclaimed. "That doesn't seem like enough money to put Allie into the nuthouse for."

Laramie and Hayes agreed. "There could be other insurance policies I'm not aware of."

"What about Megan Knight?" Jackson asked.

"Just finished college, has thousands of dollars in student loans," Laramie said. "Majored in psychology so unless she goes to grad school…"

"What do you all make of this?" Jackson asked.

"Well," his brother Laramie said. "I've always said follow the money. That will usually take you to the source of the problem."

"So WE HAVE Drew siphoning money from the business and Belinda coming into some money and Megan needing money to pay off her student loans," Jackson said. "So which of them has motive to want Allie in the nuthouse?"

"Your guess is as good as mine," Hayes said. "That photo you took from Belinda's apartment of her and Nick? The lovebirds didn't look like they were getting along."

"Wait a minute," Laramie said from the backseat. "Are you thinking with Nick gone, Drew and Belinda hooked up?"

"Good question," Jackson said.

"I've heard of stranger things happening," Hayes said.

"Or maybe it's blackmail money," Jackson said. "Maybe

Belinda has something on Drew and he's the source of the thirty-eight thousand."

"Or Drew is simply taking money from the business and giving it to Belinda to give to Nick," Hayes threw in.

"Which would mean that Drew knows Nick is alive," Jackson said.

"Or at least he has been led to believe his brother is alive according to Belinda," Hayes said.

"You two are making my head spin," Laramie cried and both brothers laughed. "No wonder I prefer facts and figures. They are so much less confusing."

"He's right," Hayes said. "It could be simple. Nick's dead, Belinda got her money from another source entirely and Drew is blowing his on beer."

As they reached Cardwell Ranch, Jackson glanced at the time. "Let's hope Allie gets some answers tonight," he said, unable to keep the worry out of his voice. "Who knows what horrors they have planned for her."

"ALLIE."

Nick's voice made Allie jump, but Katrina held tight to her hands. Goose bumps skittered over her skin as Nick spoke again.

"Allie?" His voice seemed to be coming from far away.

"We're here, Nick," Katrina said after she'd spent a good five minutes with her eyes closed, calling up Nick's spirit. "Is there something you want to say to Allie?"

She heard him groan. The sound sent her heart pounding even harder. Somehow it was more chilling than his saying her name.

"Please, Nick, do you have a message for Allie?"

Another groan, this one sounding farther away. Katrina seemed anxious as if she feared she was going to lose Nick before he said whatever it was he wanted to say.

Allie doubted that was going to happen, but maybe the

woman would try to drag this out, get more money from her by making her come back again.

She tried to pull away, but Katrina tightened her hold, pulling her forward so her elbows rested on the table.

"Nick, please, give your wife the peace she desperately needs."

Another groan. "Allie, *why?*" The last word was so ghostly that Allie felt her skin crawl. At that moment, she believed it was Nick calling to her from the grave.

"What are you asking?" Katrina called out to him.

Silence. It was so heavy that it pressed against Allie's chest until she thought she couldn't breathe.

Then a groan as forlorn as any she'd ever heard filled the small room. She shivered. "Allie," Nick said in a voice that broke. "Why did you kill me?"

Chapter Ten

Allie jerked her hands free and stumbled to her feet. She didn't realize she'd made a sound until she realized she was whimpering.

As the lights came up, she saw that Katrina was staring at her in shock as if whoever was behind this hadn't taken her into their confidence. Either that, or she was a good actress.

Allie rushed out of the room and down the hallway. Belinda wasn't in the living room where she'd been told to wait. Opening the door, Allie ran outside, stopping only when she reached Belinda's car.

None of that was real. But it had been Nick's voice; there was no doubt about that. He was either alive…or they'd somehow gotten a recording of Nick's voice. *That wasn't Nick speaking from his grave.* Intellectually, she knew that. But just hearing Nick's voice and those horrible groans…

Belinda came bursting out of the house. Allie turned to see Katrina standing at the doorway looking stunned. Or was that, too, an act?

"Allie?" Belinda ran to her looking scared. "What happened in there?"

She ignored the question. "Where were you?"

Belinda seemed taken aback by her tone, if not her question. "I had to go to the bathroom. I was just down the hall. Are you all right?"

"I want to go." Katrina was still standing in the doorway.

Allie reached for the door handle but the car was locked. "Belinda, I want to *go*."

"Okay, just a sec." She groped in her purse for her keys.

"Can't find them?" Allie taunted with a sneer. "Maybe you left them in the bathroom sink."

Belinda glanced up in surprise, frowning as if confused. "No, I have them. Honey, are you sure you're all right?"

Allie laughed. "How can you seriously ask that?"

Belinda stared at her for a moment before she opened the car doors and went around and slid behind the wheel.

They rode in silence for a few minutes before Belinda said, "I'm sorry. Clearly, you're upset. I thought—"

"What did you think?" Allie demanded.

Belinda shot her a glance before returning to her driving. "I seriously thought this might help."

"Really? Was it your idea or Nick's?"

"Nick's?" She shot her another quick look.

"I *know,* Belinda." Silence. "I know about you and Nick." Belinda started to deny it, but Allie cut her off. "You two had me going for a while, I'll give you that. I really did think I was losing my mind. But not anymore. How long have you and Nick been having an affair?"

"Allie—"

"I don't have to ask whose plan this was. It has Nick written all over it."

"Honey, I honestly don't know what you're talking about."

"No?" Allie reached into her pocket and pulled out the photo of Belinda and Nick standing next to the trailhead sign at Grouse Creek. "As you've often said, a picture is worth a thousand words."

Belinda groaned, not unlike Nick had back at the alleged psychic's. "It isn't what you think."

Allie laughed again as she put the photo back in her pocket. "It never is."

"I'm sorry." She sounded as if she were crying, but Allie could feel no compassion for her.

"What was the point of all that back there?" Allie demanded as they left the Gallatin Valley behind and entered the dark, narrow canyon.

"I swear I don't know what you're talking about. What happened in there that has you so angry and upset?"

"Don't play dumb, Belinda. It doesn't become you. But tell me, what's next?" Allie demanded. "You failed to make me crazy enough that you could take Natalie. Is it the insurance money? Is that what you're planning to use to open your own studio? But in order to get it, you're going to have to kill me. Is that the next part of your plot, Belinda?"

The woman gasped and shot her a wide-eyed look. "You sure you aren't crazy, because you are certainly talking that way. That photo of me and Nick? That was before he met and married you. I broke up with him. Why do you think he didn't like me? Why do you think he put up with me? Because I threatened to tell you about the two of us." She took a breath and let it out. "As for me trying to make you think you were crazy…" Belinda waved a hand through the air. "That's ridiculous. I'm the one who has been trying to help you. I should have told you about me and Nick, but it was water under the bridge. And Nick's insurance money? I don't need it. Remember I told you about my eccentric aunt Ethel? Well, it seems she'd been socking money away in her underwear drawer for years. Thirty-eight thousand of it was left to me, tax free. That's what I plan to use to start my own photo studio. Allie, no matter what you think, I'm your *friend*."

She had thought so, but now she didn't know what to believe. "How did you come up with the idea of me going to see Katrina?" she challenged.

Belinda drove in silence, the canyon highway a dark ribbon along the edge of the river. "I told you. I'd seen

Katrina a few times. But the idea for you to go see her so you could try to reach Nick and get closure? That was your sister *Megan*'s idea."

JACKSON FOUND HIMSELF walking the floor of his cabin until he couldn't take it anymore. Finally, he heard the sound of a vehicle, saw the headlights coming up the road and hurried down to the barn where Allie had left her van.

He waited in the shadows as both women got out of Belinda's car, neither speaking as they parted ways.

"Are you all right?" Jackson asked Allie as he stepped from the shadows. She jumped, surprised, and he mentally kicked himself for scaring her. "I'm sorry. I've been pacing the floor. I was so worried about you."

Her features softened. "I'm okay." She looked drained.

"If you don't want to talk about it tonight…"

Allie gave him a wane smile. "Natalie is staying with your family and I'm not going to be able to sleep, anyway."

"Do you mind coming up to my cabin?"

She shook her head and let him lead her up the mountainside through the pines. It was only a little after ten, but most everyone had turned in for the night so there was little light or sound on the ranch. Under the thick pine boughs, it was cool and dark and smelled of summer.

Jackson realized he was going to miss that smell when he returned to Texas. He didn't want to think about what else he might miss.

Once inside the cabin, they took a seat on the couch, turning to face each other. It was warm in the cabin away from the chill of the Montana summer night. Without prompting, Allie began to relate what had happened slowly as if she was exhausted. He didn't doubt she was.

He hated putting her through this. She told him about the ride to the psychic's and Belinda's apparent hesitancy to let her go through with it. Then she told him about Katrina and the small remote house.

"It all felt silly and like a waste of time, until I heard Nick's voice."

He looked at her and felt his heart drop. Hearing her husband's voice had clearly upset her. It surprised him that whoever was behind this had gone that far.

"You're sure it was Nick's voice."

She nodded. "It sounded as if it was far away and yet close."

"Could it have been a recording?"

"Possibly. His words were halting as if hard for him to speak and he…groaned." She shuddered. "It was an awful sound, unearthly."

"I'm so sorry. After you left, I regretted telling you to go." He sighed. "I was afraid it would just upset you and accomplish nothing."

"It gets worse. Nick…accused me of…killing him."

"*What?* That's ridiculous. I thought a grizzly killed him."

She shrugged. "The psychic believed it. You should have seen her face."

"Allie, the woman was in on it. This was just another ploy. You knew that going in."

"But I didn't know I would hear his voice. I didn't know he would ask me why I'd killed him. I didn't…" The tears came in a rush, dissolving the rest of whatever she was going to say.

Jackson pulled her to him. She buried her face into his chest. "None of this is real, Allie. Are you listening to me? None of it. They just want you to believe it is."

After a few moments, the sobs stopped. He handed her a tissue from the box by the couch and she got up and moved to the window. His cabin view was the rock cliff across the valley and a ribbon of Gallatin River below it.

As he got up, he moved to stand behind her. He could see starlight on that stretch of visible river. It shone like silver.

"If Nick is alive and I believe he is, then he has tried to do everything he can to make you think you're losing your mind. It hasn't worked. This isn't going to work, either. You're stronger than that."

"Am I?" she asked with a laugh. "I am when I'm with you, but…"

He turned her to face him. "You just needed someone to believe in you. I believe in you, Allie."

She looked up at him, her green eyes full of hope and trust and—

His gaze went to her mouth. Lowering his head, he kissed her.

A LOW MOAN escaped her lips. As he drew her closer, Allie closed her eyes, relishing in the feel of her body against his. It had been so long since a man had kissed her let alone held her. She couldn't remember the last time she'd made love. Nick had seemed to lose interest in her toward the end, which had been more than fine with her.

She banished all thoughts of Nick as she lost herself in Jackson's kiss. Her arms looped around his neck. She could feel her heart pounding next to his. Her breasts felt heavy, her nipples hard and aching as he deepened the kiss. A bolt of desire like none she'd ever known shot through her veins as he broke off the kiss to plant a trail of kisses down the column of her neck to the top of her breasts.

At her cry of arousal, Jackson pulled back to look into her eyes. "I've told myself all the reasons we shouldn't do this, but I want to make love to you."

"Yes," she said breathlessly, throwing caution to the wind. She wanted him, wanted to feel his bare skin against her own, to taste his mouth on hers again, to look up at him as he lowered himself onto her. She ached for his gentle touch, needed desperately to know the tenderness of love-making she'd never experienced with Nick but sensed in Jackson.

He swept her up in his arms and carried her to the bedroom, kicking the door closed before he carefully lowered her to the bed. She looked into his dark eyes as he lay down next to her. He touched her face with his fingertips, then slipped his hand around to the nape of her neck and drew her to him.

His kiss was slow and sensual. She could feel him fighting his own need as if determined to take it slow as he undid one button of her blouse, then another. She wanted to scream, unable to stand the barrier of their clothing between them. Grabbing his shirt, she pulled each side apart. The snaps sung as the Western shirt fell open exposing his tanned skin and the hard muscles under it.

She pressed her hands to his warm flesh as he undid the last button on her blouse. She heard his intake of breath an instant before she felt his fingertips skim across the tops of her breasts. Pushing her onto her back, he dropped his mouth to the hard points of her nipples, sucking gently through the thin, sheer fabric of her bra.

She arched against his mouth, felt him suck harder as his hand moved to the buttons of her jeans. With agonizing deliberate movements, he slowly undid the buttons of her jeans and slipped his hand beneath her panties. She cried out and fumbled at the zipper of his jeans.

"Please," she begged. "I need you."

"Not yet." His voice broke with the sound of his own need. "Not yet."

His hand dipped deeper into her panties. She arched against it, feeling the wet slickness of his fingers. He'd barely touched her when she felt the release.

"Oh, Allie," he said as if he, too, hadn't made love for a very long time. He shifted to the side to pull off her jeans and panties. She heard him shed the rest of his own clothing and then he was back, his body melding with hers in a rhythm as old as life itself.

THEY MADE LOVE twice more before the dawn. Jackson dozed off at some point, but woke to find Allie sleeping in his arms.

She looked more peaceful than she had since he'd met her. Like him, he suspected she hadn't made love with anyone for a very long time—much longer than her husband had allegedly been dead.

He cursed Nick Taylor. How could the fool not want this woman? How could the man mistreat someone so wonderful, not to mention ignore a child like Natalie? When he found the bastard...

When is it that you plan to find him?

The thought stopped him cold. There were only two more days until the wedding. He and Ford had tickets to fly out the following day.

He couldn't leave Allie now when she needed him the most. But how could he stay? He had Ford to think about. His son would be starting kindergarten next month. Jackson wasn't ready. He'd received a list from the school of the supplies his son would need, but he hadn't seen any reason to get them yet, thinking there was plenty of time. Same with the boy's new clothes.

He thought of his small ranch in Texas. Most of the land was leased, but he still had a house down there in the summer heat. He couldn't stay away indefinitely. What if he couldn't find Nick Taylor before Ford's school started?

His thoughts whirling, he looked down at Allie curled up next him and felt a pull so strong that it made him ache. What was he going to do?

Whatever it was, he couldn't think straight lying next to

this beautiful, naked woman. As he tried to pull free, she rolled away some, but didn't wake.

Slipping out of bed, he quickly dressed and stepped outside. The fresh Montana morning air helped a little. Earlier he'd heard voices down by the main house. He hoped to catch his brothers as he headed down the mountain. He needed desperately to talk to one of them, even though he had had a bad feeling what they were going to say to him. He'd been saying the same thing to himself since waking up next to Allie this morning.

ALLIE WOKE TO an empty bed. For a moment, she didn't know where she was. As last night came back to her with Jackson, she hugged herself. The lovemaking had been... amazing. This was what she'd been missing out on with Nick. Jackson had been so tender and yet so...passionate.

She lay back listening, thinking he must be in the bathroom or maybe the small kitchen. After a few minutes, she sat up. The cabin was too quiet. Surely Jackson hadn't left.

Slipping her feet over the side of the bed, she tiptoed out of the bedroom. The bathroom was empty. So was the living room and kitchen. Moving to the front window, she glanced out on the porch. No Jackson.

For a moment, she stood staring out at the view, trying to understand what this meant. Had he finally come to his senses? That was definitely one explanation.

Had he realized they had no future? That was another.

Hurrying into the bathroom, she showered, and, forced to put on the clothes she'd worn the night before, dressed. Fortunately, she'd been wearing jeans, a tank top and a blouse. She tucked the blouse into her large shoulder bag, pulled her wet hair up into a ponytail and looked at herself in the mirror.

Her cheeks were flushed from the lovemaking and the hot shower. Her skin still tingled at even the thought of

Jackson's touch. She swallowed. Hadn't she warned herself last night of all the reasons they shouldn't make love?

At a knock on the cabin door, she jumped. Her heart leaped to her throat as she saw a dark, large shadow move on the porch beyond the curtains. Jackson wouldn't knock. Maybe it was one of his brothers.

She held her breath, hoping he would go away. She didn't want to be caught here, even though she knew his brothers wouldn't tell anyone.

Another knock.

"Jackson?" Drew Taylor's voice made her cringe. She put her hand over her mouth to keep from crying out in surprise. "I need to check something in your cabin." She heard him try the door and felt her heart drop. What if Jackson had left the door open?

She was already backing up, frantically trying to decide where she could hide, when she heard Drew try the knob. Locked.

He swore, thumped around on the porch for a moment then retreated down the steps.

Allie finally had to let out the breath she'd been holding. If Drew had caught her here… What would he have done? Tell Nick. But what would a man who had faked his death do to stop his plan from working? She thought of Jackson and felt her heart drop. She'd put Jackson's life in danger, as well.

She waited until she was sure Drew had gone before she cautiously moved to the door, opened it and peered out. She could see nothing but pines as she slipped out and hurried across the mountainside, planning to slip into the barn as if she'd come to work early.

With luck, no one would be the wiser.

Allie didn't see Drew. But he saw her.

Chapter Eleven

Dana was sitting on the porch as Jackson approached the house. She motioned for him to join her.

"Where is everyone?" he asked, taking the rocker next to her.

"Early morning ride. Hud took everyone including the kids. Quiet, isn't it?" She glanced over at him. "How are you this morning?"

"Fine." He would have said great, but he had a bad feeling where Dana was headed with the conversation.

"I'm worried about Allie," she said, looking past him to the mountainside.

He glanced back toward the cabins in time to see Allie hurrying toward the barn from the direction of his cabin.

"Is she all right?"

In truth, he didn't know how she was. He regretted leaving before she'd awakened, but he'd needed to get out of there. "I—"

"She's been through so much. I would hate to see her get hurt. Wouldn't you?"

He felt as if she'd slapped him. He closed his eyes for a moment before he turned to look at her. "I told myself not to get involved, but…"

"So now you are involved?" Dana frowned. "She's in trouble, isn't she?"

Jackson nodded. "I have to help her." Even if it meant

staying in Montana longer, he couldn't abandon her. Isn't that what had scared the hell out of him when he'd awakened this morning? He was in deep, how deep, he didn't want to admit. "She's going through some things right now but she's working so hard on the wedding, it will be fine."

Dana studied him openly. "You care about her."

"I'm not going to hurt her."

"I hope not." She gave him a pat on the shoulder as she rose and went inside the house.

Jackson sat looking after his cousin, mentally kicking himself. *"What the hell are you doing?"*

"I was going to ask you the same thing." Laramie came walking up.

As he climbed the porch, Jackson said, "I thought you went riding with the others."

"I've been working," his brother said as he took a seat next to him. He shook his head. "I hope you know what you're doing, Jackson." He sighed and pulled out a sheet of paper. "Allie's mother spent the last seven years of her life in a mental institution. Paranoid schizophrenia."

As ALLIE SLIPPED into the barn, she was surprised to see Belinda setting up her gear for a shoot. She'd half expected Belinda to be gone after their argument last night. In fact, Allie had almost called several photographers she knew to see if they could possibly fill in at the last minute.

"So you're still here," she said as she approached Belinda.

"Where did you think I would be?"

"I wasn't sure. I thought you might have quit."

Belinda shook her head. "You really do have so little faith in me. I'm amazed. I'm the one who has stuck by you all these years. I'm sorry about…everything. But I'm here to do a job I love. Surely you understand that."

Allie did and said as much. "If I've underestimated you—"

Her friend laughed. "Or overestimated me given that you

think I'm capable of some diabolical plot to destroy you. And what? Steal your cabin on the river? Steal Nick's insurance money?" Her eyes widened. "Or was it steal Natalie?" Belinda looked aghast. "Oh, Allie, no wonder you're so upset. I get it now."

She felt tears rush her eyes as Belinda pulled her into a stiff, awkward hug.

"No matter what you believe, I'm still your friend," Belinda said as she broke the embrace and left the barn, passing Megan who looked bewildered as she came in.

Allie waited until she and Megan were alone before she spoke to her stepsister about what Belinda had told her. She didn't want to believe Megan had anything to do with the psychic or what had happened last night. Either Belinda was lying or there had to be another explanation.

"I need to ask you something."

"You sound so serious," Megan said. "What is it?"

"Was it your idea for me to see the psychic?"

Megan frowned. "I guess I was the one who suggested it. When Belinda told me about some of the things you'd been going through, I thought— Allie, why are you so upset?"

Allie had turned away, unable to look at her sister. Now she turned back, just as unable to hide her disappointment. "Why would you do that?"

"I just told you. I thought it would help."

"Trying to reach Nick on…the other side?" she demanded. "You can't be serious."

"A girl I knew at college lost her mother before the two of them could work some things out. She went to a psychic and was able to put some of the issues to rest. I thought…" Her gaze locked with her sister's. "I wanted to help you. I couldn't bear the things Belinda was telling me. It sounded as if you'd been going through hell. If I was wrong, I'm sorry."

Allie studied her for a moment. "You would never betray me, would you, Megan?"

"What a strange question to ask me."

"This past year since you came into my life and Natalie's… It's meant so much to both of us. Tell me you wouldn't betray that trust."

Megan frowned. "Does this have something to do with Jackson Cardwell? Is he the one putting these ideas in your head?"

"He has a theory about the so-called incidents I've been having," Allie confided. "He thinks someone is trying to make me think I'm crazy in order to take Natalie from me."

"That sounds…crazy in itself. Allie, I hate to say this, but you are starting to sound like your—"

"Don't say it," Allie cried. Wasn't that her real underlying fear, the one that had haunted her her whole life? That she was becoming sick like her mother? She rubbed a hand over the back of her neck. What was she sure of right now? She'd thought Jackson, but after this morning… "I know it sounds crazy, but if it's true, I have to find out who is behind it."

"And Jackson is *helping* you?" Megan said and frowned. "Or is he complicating things even more? You aren't…falling for him, are you?"

JACKSON WASN'T SURE what he was going to say to Allie. He felt like a heel for leaving her alone this morning. She must be furious with him. No, he thought, not Allie. She would be hurt, and that made him feel worse than if she was angry.

He headed for the barn to apologize to her. Once inside, though, he didn't see Allie.

"She said she had to run an errand," Megan told him with a shrug.

Glancing outside, he saw her van still parked where it had been last night. "Did she go on foot?"

"Her brother-in-law offered her a ride."

"Drew?" Jackson felt his heart race at the thought of Allie alone with that man. "Do you know where they went?"

Megan shook her head and kept working.

"You don't like me," he said, stepping farther into the barn. "Why is that?"

"I don't think you're good for my sister."

"Based on what?" he had to ask. "We have barely met."

"She told me about this crazy idea you have that someone is causing these incidents she's been having."

"You disagree?"

Megan gave him an impatient look. "I know the Taylors. The last thing they want is a five-year-old to raise."

"So you think what's been happening to Allie is all in her head?"

She put down what she'd been working on and gave him her full attention for the first time. "You just met her. You don't know anything about her. I love my stepsister, but I don't think she has been completely honest with you. Did you know that her mother spent her last years in a mental hospital? Or that she killed herself?"

"You aren't trying to tell me it runs in the family."

Megan raised a brow. "Allie's been through a lot. She has some issues she hasn't gotten past, including the fact that she wanted her husband gone. So she already told you about that, huh?" He nodded. "Did she also tell you that she bought a gun just before Nick went up into the mountains? That's right. I wonder what happened to it." She shrugged. "Like I said, I love Allie and Nat, but I also know that Allie hated her husband and would have done anything to escape him."

ALLIE HAD BEEN on her way to her van when Drew had suddenly appeared next to her.

"Where you off to?" he'd asked.

"I just have to pick up some ribbon at the store," she'd said, trying to act normal. What a joke. She hadn't felt *normal* in so long, she'd forgotten what it felt like. Worse, she feared that Drew would find out about last night. The Taylors wouldn't hesitate to use it against her, claiming it proved what a terrible mother she was.

Allie felt guilty enough. Her husband had been dead only months and here she was making love with another man. Did it matter that she hadn't loved Nick for years? She had a child to think about and Jackson Cardwell would be leaving in two days' time. Then what?

It would be just her and Nat and the Taylors.

"I'll give you a ride," Drew said. She started to argue but he stopped her. "It would be stupid to take your van when I'm going that way, anyway. You pick up your ribbon. I'll pick up the chalk I need next door at the hardware store. We'll be back here before you know it."

All her instincts warned her not to get into the pickup with him, but she couldn't think of a reason not to accept the ride without acting paranoid. Did she really think he would take her somewhere other than the store and what? Attack her?

She climbed into the passenger side of the pickup and remembered something Nick had said not long before he'd left to go hunting that day.

"You're so damned trusting, Allie. I worry about you. Don't you get tired of being so nice?" He'd laughed and pretended he was joking as he pulled her close and kissed the top of her head. "Don't change. It's refreshing."

It also had made it easier for him to control her.

"You want to know something crazy?" Drew said as he started the engine and drove down the road toward Big Sky. "When I got here this morning, your van was where you'd left it last night. There was dew on the window. I checked the motor. It hadn't been moved and even more interesting, you were nowhere to be found."

She didn't look at him as he roared down the road. Ahead

she could see the bridge that spanned the Gallatin River. Why hadn't she listened to her instincts and not gotten into the vehicle with Drew?

"It was like a mystery. I love mysteries. Did I ever tell you that?"

A recent rainstorm had washed out some of the road just before the bridge, leaving deep ruts that were to be filled this afternoon. Couldn't have the wedding guests being jarred by the ruts.

"I saw you come out of Jackson Cardwell's cabin this morning." Drew swore as he braked for the ruts. "You slut." He started to backhand her, but had to brake harder as he hit the first rut so his hand went back to the wheel before it reached its mark. "How could you screw—"

Allie unsnapped her seat belt and grabbed the door handle.

As the door swung open, Drew hit the brakes even harder, slamming her into the door as she jumped. She hit the soft earth at the side of the road, lost her footing and fell into the ditch.

Drew stopped the truck. She heard his door open and the shocks groan as he climbed out. By then she was on her feet and headed into the pines next to the road, running, even though her right ankle ached.

"Allie!" Drew yelled from the roadbed. "You could have killed yourself. You're crazy, you know that?"

She kept running through the pines. Her brother-in-law was right. She had been stupid. Stupid to get into the truck with him when all her instincts had been telling her not to, and crazy to jump out.

Behind her, she heard the truck engine rev, then the pickup rumble over the bridge. She slowed to catch her breath then limped the rest of the way back to the barn, telling herself she was through being naive and trusting.

JACKSON DIDN'T SEE Allie until that evening at the wedding rehearsal so he had no chance to get her alone. "We need to talk," he whispered in those few seconds he managed to get her somewhat alone.

She met his gaze. "Look, I think I already know what you're going to say."

"I doubt that." She wore a multicolored skirt and top that accentuated her lush body. "You look beautiful. That top brings out the green in your eyes."

"Thank you." Something glinted in those eyes for a moment. "Jackson—"

"I know. This isn't the place. But can we please talk later? It's important."

She nodded, though reluctantly.

He mentally kicked himself for running out on her this morning as he stood there, wanting to say more, but not able to find the right words.

Allie excused herself. He watched her head for the preacher as the rehearsal was about to begin. Was she limping?

All day he'd stewed over what Megan had told him. She was wrong about Allie, but he could understand why she felt the way she did. Maybe she really did love her sister. Or maybe not.

Belinda was busy behind her camera, shooting as they all went to their places. As one of the best men, Jackson was in a position to watch the others. He hadn't seen much of Sarah Taylor. But Sarah, her mother and brother would be at the rehearsal dinner tonight. He watched Sarah enter the barn and start up the aisle toward the steps to where the preacher was standing along with the best men and the groom.

An overweight woman with dull, brown hair pulled severely back from her face, Sarah seemed somewhere else, oblivious to what was happening. Either that or bored. Four more bridesmaids entered and took their places.

Harlan and Angus broke into "Here Comes the Bride" on their guitars and Lily came out of a small-framed building next to the meadow with her father and mother. Jackson hadn't met either of them yet but he wanted to laugh when he saw them looking as if in horror. Lily was smiling from ear to ear. So was her brother Ace from the sidelines. But clearly her parents hadn't expected this kind of wedding for their only daughter.

Jackson looked over at Allie. She really was beautiful. She glanced to the parking lot and quickly looked away as if she'd seen something that frightened her.

He followed her gaze. Drew Taylor stood lounging against his pickup, a malicious smirk on his face as if he was up to something.

THE REHEARSAL WENT off without a hitch. Allie tried to breathe a sigh of relief. Dana had booked an Italian restaurant in Bozeman for the night of the rehearsal dinner. "I know it's not the way things are normally done," she'd said with a laugh. "But Lily and I discussed it."

Dana had insisted anyone involved in the wedding had to be there so that meant Allie and Natalie as well as Megan and Belinda.

They'd just gotten to the restaurant when Allie heard a strident voice behind her say, "There you are."

She bristled but didn't turn, putting off facing her mother-in-law as long as possible.

"Sarah thinks you're avoiding us," Mildred said. "But why would you do that?"

Allie turned, planting a smile on her face. "I wouldn't."

"Hmmm," her mother-in-law said. She gave Allie the once-over. "You look different."

Allie remembered that she was wearing one of two

outfits that she hadn't taken back to the store. This one was a multicolored top and skirt that Jackson had said brought out the green in her eyes. She loved it and while it was more expensive than she could really afford, she'd needed something to wear tonight.

"Where did you get that outfit?" Mildred asked, eyeing her with suspicion.

"I found it in my closet," Allie said honestly.

"Really?"

Allie felt a hand take hers and looked up to see Jackson.

"I saved you a spot down here," he said and led her to the other end of the table, away from the Taylors.

Dana had insisted that there be no prearranged seating. "Let everyone sit where they want. I like people to be comfortable." Lily had seemed relieved that she could sit by Tag, away from her parents.

Allie was grateful to Jackson for saving her. Dinner was served and the conversation around the table was light with lots of laughter and joking. She was glad Jackson didn't try to talk to her about last night.

It had been a mistake in so many ways. But tomorrow after the wedding, they would say goodbye and he and Ford would fly out the next day. She told herself that once the wedding was over, everything would be all right.

A part of her knew she was only kidding herself. There hadn't been any more incidents, no misplaced keys, no Nick sightings, no "black cat" scares and that almost worried her. What had changed? Or was Nick and whomever he had helping him just waiting to ambush her?

She had a feeling that the séance with the psychic hadn't produced the results they'd wanted. Now she, too, was waiting. Waiting for the other shoe to drop.

Just let it drop after the wedding, she prayed. Jackson and Ford would be back in Texas. Whatever was planned for her, she felt she could handle it once this job was over.

The one thing Jackson had done was made her feel stronger, more sure of herself. He'd also reminded her that she was a woman with needs that had long gone unmet until last night.

"Stop telling stories on me," Tag pleaded at the dinner table across from her. "Lily is going to change her mind about marrying me."

"Not a chance, cowboy," Lily said next to him before she'd kissed him to hoots and hollers.

Even Sarah seemed to be enjoying herself with the other bridesmaids since they had all worked together at Lily's brother's bar.

Allie avoided looking down the table to see how the Taylors were doing. She was so thankful to be sitting as far away from them as possible, especially Drew. To think that she'd trusted him and thought he'd really had her and Nat's best interest at heart. She'd felt his eyes on her all night. The few times she'd met his gaze, he'd scowled at her.

She glanced over at the children's table to see her daughter also enjoying herself. Dana's sister Stacy had the children at a separate table. Allie saw that her daughter was being on her best behavior. So ladylike, she was even using the manners Allie had taught her. She felt a swell of pride and told herself that she and Natalie were going to be all right no matter what happened after the wedding.

To her surprise, her eyes welled with tears and she quickly excused herself to go to the ladies' room. The bathroom was past an empty section of the restaurant, then down a long hallway. She was glad that no one had followed her. She needed a few minutes alone.

Inside the bathroom, she pulled herself together. Last night with Jackson had meant more to her than she'd admitted. It had hurt this morning when he hadn't been there, but she could understand why he'd panicked. Neither of them took that kind of intimacy lightly.

Feeling better, she left the bathroom. As she reached the

empty section of the restaurant, Drew stepped in front of her, startling her. She could smell the alcohol on him. The way he was standing… She recognized that stance after five years of being married to his brother.

Drew was looking for a fight. How had she thought the brothers were different? Because she hadn't seen this side of Drew. Until now.

"You *jumped* out of my truck. What the hell was that? Do I scare you, Allie?" he asked, slurring his words and blocking her way.

"Please, Drew, don't make a scene."

He laughed. "Oh, you don't want Dana to know that you slept with her cousin?"

"Drew—"

"Don't bother to lie to me," he said as he stepped toward her, shoving her back. "I *saw* you." His voice broke. "How can you do this to my brother?"

"Nick's…gone."

"And forgotten. Is that it?" He forced her back against the wall, caging her with one hand on each side of her.

"Please, Drew—"

"If Nick really was out of the picture…" He belched. "You have to know I've always wanted you," he said drunkenly. Before she could stop him, he bent down and tried to kiss her.

She turned her head to the side. He kissed her hair, then angrily grabbed her jaw in one hand. His fingers squeezed painfully as he turned her to face him.

"What? Am I not good enough for you?"

"Drew—"

Suddenly he was jerked away. Allie blinked as Jackson hauled back and swung. His fist connected with Drew's jaw and he went down hard, crashing into a table.

"Are you all right?" Jackson asked, stepping to her.

She nodded and glanced at her brother-in-law. He was

trying to get up, but he seemed to take one look at Jackson and decided to stay down.

"You'll pay for that!" he threatened as she and Jackson headed back toward their table. Allie knew he wasn't talking to Jackson. She would pay.

"If he bothers you again—" Jackson said as if reading her mind.

"Don't worry about me."

"How can I not?" he demanded. "That was about me, wasn't it?"

"Drew was just looking for a reason."

"And I provided it."

"He saw me leaving your cabin this morning," she said. "I don't think he's told anyone, but he will. I just wanted to warn you. I'm afraid what Nick might do to you."

"Allie, I don't give a damn about any of that. What I'm sorry about was leaving you this morning," he said, bringing her up short as he stopped and turned her to face him. "There is so much I want to say to you—"

"Oh, there you are," Mildred Taylor said as she approached. "I was just looking for Drew. I thought you might have seen him. Allie, you look terrible. I knew this job was going to be too much for you."

Natalie and Ford came running toward them. Mildred began to say something about giving Allie and Nat a ride home, but then Drew appeared, rubbing his jaw.

"Drew, whatever happened to you?" Mildred cried.

"I still need to talk to you," Jackson whispered to Allie, who was bending down to catch her daughter up into her arms.

"After the wedding," she said as she lifted Natalie, hugging her tightly. "Tonight I just need to take my daughter home."

Jackson wanted to stop her. But she was right. The wedding was the important thing right now. After that…

Chapter Twelve

Wedding Day. Allie woke at the crack of dawn. She couldn't help being nervous and excited. The wedding was to be held in a beautiful meadow near the house. Those attending had been told to wear Western attire as the seating at the wedding would be hay bales.

Drew had constructed an arch for the bride and groom to stand under with the preacher. Allie had walked through everything with the bride and groom, the caterer and the musicians. The barn was ready for the reception that would follow. But she still wanted to get to the ranch early to make sure she hadn't forgotten anything.

The last few days had felt like a roller-coaster ride. Today, she needed calm. Jackson hadn't tried to contact her after she and Natalie left the restaurant with Dana and family last night and she was glad. She needed time with her daughter.

Natalie hadn't slept in her own bed for several nights now. Allie made sure her daughter's window was locked as she put her to bed. She checked the other windows and the door. Then, realizing that any of the Taylors could have a key to her cabin, she pushed a straight-back chair under the doorknob.

She and Natalie hadn't been disturbed all night. At least not by intruders. In bed last night, Allie couldn't help but think about Jackson. And Nick.

"Please, just let me get through this wedding," she'd prayed and had finally fallen asleep.

Now as she drove into the ranch, she saw that Dana and the kids were waiting for Natalie.

"We have a fun morning planned," Dana said with a wink. "You don't have to worry about anything today."

Allie wished that was true. She looked down at the meadow to see that Megan was up early. She was sitting on a hay bale looking as if she were staring at the arch. Imagining her own wedding? Allie wondered as she approached.

"Good morning," she said and joined her sister on the bale.

"It's perfect. Drew really did do a good job," Megan said.

The arch had been made out of natural wood that blended in beautifully with its surroundings. Allie had asked Lily if she wanted it decorated with flowers.

"There will be enough wildflowers in the meadow and I will be carrying a bouquet. I think that is more than enough."

She had agreed and was happy that Lily preferred the more minimalist look.

"Have you been up to the barn?" Allie asked.

"Not yet." Megan finally looked over at her. "How are you?"

"Fine."

Her sister eyed her. "You can lean on me. I'm here for you and Natalie."

Allie hugged her, closing her eyes and praying it was true. She couldn't bear the thought of Megan betraying not only her but Natalie, as well.

Together they walked up to the barn. Allie turned on the lights and gasped.

JACKSON HAD TOSSED and turned all night—after he'd finally dropped off to sleep. He felt as if he'd let Allie down. Or maybe worse, gotten involved with her in the first place, knowing he would be leaving soon.

She wasn't out of the woods yet. She had to know that whoever was messing with her mind wasn't through. He still believed it had to be Nick. He had the most to gain. It scared Jackson to think that whoever was behind this might try to use Tag's wedding to put the last nail in Allie's coffin, so to speak.

His fear, since realizing what was going on, was that if they couldn't drive her crazy, they might actually try to kill her.

He was just getting dressed when he heard the knock at his cabin door. His mood instantly lifted as he thought it might be Allie. She'd said she would talk to him *after* the wedding. Maybe she had changed her mind. He sure hoped so.

Jackson couldn't hide his disappointment when he opened the door and saw his brothers standing there.

"I found something that I think might interest you," Laramie said and he stepped back to let them enter.

"Shouldn't you be getting ready for your wedding?" he asked Tag, who laughed and said, "I have been getting ready for months now. I just want this damned wedding over."

They took a seat while he remained standing. From the expressions on their faces, they hadn't brought good news.

"Nick and his brother, Drew, took out life insurance policies on each other through their construction business," Laramie said.

"That isn't unusual, right?" he asked.

"They purchased million-dollar policies and made each other the beneficiary, but Nick purchased another half million and made Allie the beneficiary."

Jackson let out a low whistle. "All Allie knew about was the hundred-thousand-dollar policy." He saw Hayes lift a brow. "She didn't kill her husband."

"Whether she knew or not about the policies, I believe it supports your theory that Nick is alive and trying to get that money," Laramie said.

"It hasn't paid out yet, right?"

"She should be getting the checks next week."

Jackson raked a hand through his hair. Allie was bound to have been notified. Maybe it had slipped her mind. "You're sure she is the beneficiary?"

Laramie nodded.

"Who gets the money if Allie is declared incompetent?"

"Her daughter, Natalie."

Jackson groaned. "Then this is why Nick is trying to have Allie committed. He, and whoever he is working with, would get the money and Natalie."

"Only if Nick is alive and *stays* dead," Hayes pointed out.

"If Nick stays dead the money would be used at the discretion of Natalie's *guardian*."

Jackson looked at his brother, an ache starting at heart level. "Who is her guardian?"

"Megan Knight. The policy was changed eight months ago—just before Nick Taylor went up into the mountains hunting and a guardian was added."

ALLIE COULDN'T EVEN scream. Her voice had caught in her throat at the sight in the barn. Last night when she'd left, the barn had been ready for the reception except for putting out the fresh vases of flowers at each setting. The tables had been covered with the checked tablecloths and all the overhead lanterns had been in place along with the decorations on the walls and in the rafters.

"Oh, my word," Megan said next to her.

Allie still couldn't speak. Someone had ripped the tablecloths from the tables and piled them in the middle of the dance floor. The old boots that served as centerpieces that would hold the fresh flowers were arranged on the floor in a circle as if the invisible people in them were dancing.

Megan was the first one to move. She rushed to the tablecloths and, bending down, picked up the top one. "They've all been shredded." She turned to look at Allie, concern in her gaze.

"You can't think I did this."

Her sister looked at the tablecloth in her hand before returning her gaze to Allie. "This looks like a cry for help."

Allie shook her head. "It's someone who hates me."

"Hates you? Oh, Allie."

"What's happened?"

She swung around to see Jackson standing in the doorway. Tears filled her eyes. She wanted to run out the barn door and keep running, but he stepped to her and took one of her hands.

"I was afraid they weren't done with you," he said. "How bad is it?" he asked Megan.

"The tablecloths are ruined. Fortunately, whoever did this didn't do anything to the lanterns or the other decorations in the rafters. Probably couldn't reach them since the ladders have all been packed away." This last was directed at Allie, her meaning clear.

"Tag already ordered tablecloths for the restaurant," Jackson said, pulling out his cell phone. "I'll see if they've come in. We can have this fixed quickly if they have." He spoke into the phone for a moment. When he disconnected, he smiled at Allie and said, "Tag will bring up the red-checked cloths right away. With their help, we'll have it fixed before anyone else hears about it."

Allie went weak with relief as he quickly got rid of the ruined tablecloths and Tag showed up with new ones from the restaurant. With the Cardwell brothers' help, the problem was solved within minutes.

"I want at least two people here watching this barn until the wedding is over," Jackson said.

"I'll talk to Dana and see if there are a couple of ranch hands who can help," Laramie said.

"That really isn't necessary," Megan said. "I will stay here to make sure nothing else happens."

Jackson shook his head. "I'm not taking any chances. I'll feel better if you aren't left alone here. Whoever is doing this… Well, I think it might get dangerous before it's over."

"Why don't you just admit that you think I'm involved in this," Megan said and looked sadly at her sister. "Apparently, you aren't the only one who's paranoid." She sighed. "Whatever you need me to do. I don't want anything to spoil this wedding."

JACKSON HAD PLANNED to talk to Allie about the insurance policies, but he realized it could wait until after the wedding. Allie's spirit seemed buoyed once the barn was ready again and a ranch hand stayed behind with Megan to make sure nothing else went wrong.

He was having a hard time making sense of the insurance policy news. Why would Nick Taylor change the guardian from his brother to Allie's stepsister, Megan? The obvious answer would be if the two were in cahoots.

That would break Allie's heart, but a part of her had to know that her sister thought all of this was in her head. Megan had given him the impression that she was ready to step in as more than Natalie's guardian.

Jackson reminded himself that it was his brother's wedding day. As much as he didn't like weddings and hadn't attended one since his marriage had ended, he tried to concentrate on being there for Tag. He couldn't help being in awe as Allie went into wedding-planner mode. He admired the way she handled herself, even with all the stress she was under in her personal life. The day took on a feeling of celebration; after all it was the Fourth of July.

At the house, Allie made sure they were all ready, the men dressed in Western attire and boots, before she went to help the bride. Jackson had seen his father and uncle with their guitars heading for the meadow. They would be playing the "Wedding March" as well as accompanying several singers who would be performing. He just hoped everything went smoothly for Tag and Lily's sake, as well as Allie's.

"Look who's here," Laramie said, sounding too cheerful.

Jackson turned to see his mother on the arm of a nice-looking gray-haired Texas oilman. Franklin Wellington IV had oil written all over him. Jackson tried not to hold it against the man as he and his brothers took turns hugging their mother and wishing her well before shaking hands with Franklin.

His mother *did* look deliriously happy, Jackson had to admit, and Franklin was downright friendly and nice.

"Time to go," Allie said, sticking her head into the room where he and his brothers had been waiting.

Jackson introduced her to his mother and Franklin. He saw his mother lift a brow in the direction of Laramie and groaned inwardly. She would trust Laramie to tell her why she was being introduced to the wedding planner.

Allie didn't notice the interplay as she smiled at Tag. "Your bride looks absolutely beautiful and you don't look so bad yourself."

She was quite pretty, as well, in her navy dress with the white piping. She'd pulled her hair up. Silver earrings dangled at her lobes. She looked professional and yet as sexy as any woman he'd ever known. He felt a sense of pride in her, admiring her strength as well as her beauty. She'd been through so much.

Hell, he thought as he took his place, I *am* falling for her. That realization shook him to the soles of his boots.

In the meadow, his father and uncle began to play the "Wedding March" at Allie's nod. Compared to most, the wedding was small since Tag and Lily knew few people in Big Sky. But old canyon friends had come who had known the Cardwells, Savages and Justices for years.

As Lily appeared, Jackson agreed with Allie. She looked beautiful. He heard his brother's intake of breath and felt his heart soar at the look on Tag's face when he saw his bride-to-be. For a man who had sworn off weddings, Jackson had to admit, he was touched by this one.

The ceremony was wonderfully short, the music perfect and when Tag kissed the bride, Jackson felt his gaze searching for Allie. She was standing by a tree at the edge of the meadow. She was smiling, her expression one of happy contentment. She'd gotten them married.

Now if they could just get through the reception without any more trouble, he thought.

AT THE RECEPTION, Jackson watched the Taylor family sitting at a table away from the others. Mildred had a smile plastered on her face, but behind it he could see that she was sizing up everyone in the room. Her insecurities were showing as she leaned over and said something to her daughter.

Whatever her mother said to her, Sarah merely nodded. She didn't seem to have any interest in the guests, unlike her mother. Instead, she was watching Allie. What was it that Jackson caught in her gaze? Jealousy? Everyone at the wedding had been complimenting Allie on the job she'd done. Sarah couldn't have missed that.

Nor, according to Hud, had Sarah ever been married. She had to be in her late thirties. Was she thinking that it might never happen for her? Or was she content with living next to her mother and basically becoming her mother's caregiver?

Sarah reached for one of the boot-shaped cookies with Tag and Lily's wedding date on them. Her mother slapped her hand, making Sarah scowl at her before she took two cookies.

He wondered what grudges bubbled just below the surface in any family situation, let alone a wedding. Weddings, he thought, probably brought out the best and worst of people, depending how happy or unhappy you were in your own life.

As happy as he was for Tag, it still reminded him of his own sorry marriage. What did this wedding do to the Taylor clan? he wondered as he studied them. It certainly didn't seem to be bringing out any joy, that was for sure.

But his side of the family were having a wonderful time. He watched his brother Tag dancing with his bride. Their mother was dancing with her new husband, both women looking radiant. It really was a joyous day. Dana and Hud had all the kids out on the floor dancing.

Jackson thought the only thing that could make this day better would be if he could get the wedding planner to dance with him.

ALLIE TRIED TO breathe a little easier. The wedding had gone off without a hitch. Lily had been exquisite and Tag as handsome as any Cardwell, which was saying a lot. Allie had teared up like a lot of the guests when the two had exchanged their vows. She'd always loved weddings. This one would remain her favorite for years to come.

When the bride and groom kissed, she'd seen Jackson looking for her. Their eyes had locked for a long moment. She'd pulled away first, a lump in her throat, an ache in her heart. The wedding was over. There was nothing keeping Jackson and Ford in Montana.

Whoever had been trying to gaslight her, as Jackson had called it, hadn't succeeded. Maybe now they would give up trying. She certainly hoped so. If Nick was alive, then she should find out soon. The insurance check for the hundred thousand would be deposited into her account next week.

She'd already made plans for most of it to go into an interest-bearing account for Natalie's college.

Allie wondered what would happen then. If Nick was alive, would he just show up at her door? Or would the media be involved with reporters and photographers snapping photos of him outside the cabin as he returned from his ordeal?

All she knew was that the only way Nick could get his hands on the insurance money would be if he killed her. That thought unnerved her as she surveyed the reception. Belinda was busy shooting each event along with some candid shots of guests. Allie had to hand it to her, she appeared to be doing a great job.

Everything looked beautiful. Megan had taken care of the flowers in the boot vases, put the attendees' gifts on the tables and made sure the bar was open and serving. Appetizers were out. Allie checked to make sure the caterer was ready then looked around for her daughter. Nat was with the other kids and Dana. Allie had bought her a special dress for the wedding. Natalie looked beautiful and she knew it because she seemed to glow.

Her tomboy daughter loved getting dressed up. She smiled at the thought. She was thinking that they should dress up more when Mildred Taylor let out a scream at a table near the dance floor and stumbled to her feet.

Allie saw that she was clutching her cell phone, her other hand over her mouth.

"What is it?" Dana demanded, moving quickly to the Taylors' table.

"It's *my Nicky,*" Mildred cried, her gaze going to Allie, who froze thinking it was already happening. She was so sure she knew what her mother-in-law was about to say, that she thought she'd misunderstood.

"His body has been found," Mildred managed to say between sobs. She cried harder. "They say he was *murdered.*"

Chapter Thirteen

Pandemonium broke out with Mildred Taylor shrieking uncontrollably and everyone trying to calm her down.

Jackson looked over at Allie. All the color had bled from her face. He moved quickly to her. "Let's get you out of here," he said, taking her hand. "You look like you could use some fresh air."

"I'll see to Natalie," Dana said nearby as she motioned for Jackson and Allie to go.

Allie looked as if she were in shock. "It just won't end," she said in a breathless rush as he ushered her outside. "It just won't end."

"I'm so sorry," Jackson said, his mind reeling, as well.

"I was so sure he was *alive*." She met his gaze. "I thought…"

"We both thought he was alive. I'm as floored as you are." He realized that wasn't possible. Nick Taylor had been her husband, even if he had been a bad one, she would still be shocked and upset by this news. He was the father of her child.

"Nick was *murdered*? How is that possible? They found his backpack and his gun and the grizzly tracks."

"We need to wait until we have all the details," he said as his brothers Hayes and Laramie joined them.

"We're headed down to the police station now," Hayes said. "I'll let you know as soon as I have any information."

"Thank you." Jackson swallowed the lump in his throat. His brothers had been so great through his divorce and custody battle, and now this. He couldn't have been more grateful for them.

"The police will be looking for me," Allie said, her eyes widening.

He saw the fear in her eyes and at first had misunderstood it then he remembered what had happened at the psychic's. "No one believes you killed your husband."

"*Someone* already does."

"That's crazy. How could whoever was behind the séance know that Nick was even murdered unless they did the killing?"

She shook her head. "Mildred has blamed me for his death all along. Belinda thought I drove him to kill himself. Don't you see? They didn't have to know it was true. They just wanted me to feel responsible. Now that it *is* true… Even dead, he's going to ruin my life."

The last of the sun's rays slipped behind the mountains to the west, pitching the canyon in cool twilight. Inside the barn, the reception was continuing thanks to Megan and Dana, who had taken over.

"I need to go back in."

"No." Jackson stopped her with a hand on her arm. "You did a great job. No one expects you to do any more. You don't have to worry about any of that."

She met his gaze. "I don't understand what's going on."

"My brothers will find out. Allie, I'm sorry I left you the other morning. I…panicked. But I'm not leaving you now."

Allie shook her head and took a step back from him. "This isn't your problem. You should never have gotten involved because it's only going to get worse."

He remembered what Laramie had told him about the insurance policy and realized she was right. The money would definitely interest the police. He looked toward the barn. Some guests had come out into the evening air to admire the sunset.

"Please, come up to my cabin with me so we have some privacy. There's something important I need to tell you." He saw her expression and realized that she'd misunderstood.

She looked toward the barn, then up the mountain in the direction of his cabin.

"I just need to talk to you," he assured her.

"That wasn't what I…" She met his gaze. "Jackson, I've caused you enough grief as it is. If the Taylors come looking for me—"

"Let me worry about your in-laws. As for Drew, he won't be bothering you as long as I'm around."

She smiled at that. They both knew that once he left she would again be at the mercy of not just Drew but also the rest of the Taylor family.

He wanted to tell her he wouldn't leave her. But he couldn't make that promise, could he?

She was on her own and she knew it.

"Come on," he said and reached for her hand.

DARKNESS CAME ON quickly in the narrow canyon because of the steep mountains on each side. Allie could hear the fireworks vendors getting ready for the wedding grand finale and glanced at her watch. They were right on time. Maybe she wasn't as necessary as she'd thought since everything seemed to be going on schedule without her.

Overhead the pines swayed in the summer night's breeze. Jackson was so close she could smell his woodsy aftershave and remember his mouth on hers. The perfect summer night. Wasn't that what she'd been thinking earlier before her mother-in-law had started screaming?

Nick was dead. Murdered.

For days now she'd believed he was alive and behind all

the weird things that had been happening to her. Now how did she explain it?

Jackson stopped on the porch. "We can talk privately here, if you would be more comfortable not going inside." He must have seen the answer in her expression because he let go of her hand and moved to the edge of the porch.

Inside the cabin she would remember the two of them making love in his big, log-framed bed. Her skin ached at the memory of his touch.

"Allie, I hate to bring this up now, but the police will ask you…" He leaned against the porch railing, Allie just feet away. "Were you aware that your husband and brother-in-law took out life insurance policies on each other when they started their construction business?"

"No, but what does that have to do with me?"

"They purchased million-dollar policies and made the other brother the beneficiary, but Nick purchased another half million and made you beneficiary. He never mentioned it to you?"

She shook her head, shocked by the news and even more shocked by how it would look. "You think a million and a half dollars in insurance money gives me a motive for killing him."

"I don't, but I think the police might, given that just before your husband went up into the mountains on his hunting trip, he changed the beneficiary of his million-dollar insurance policy from Drew to you."

Allie didn't think anything else could surprise her. "Why would he do that?" Her eyes filled with tears as a reason came to her. She moved to the opposite railing and looked out across the darkening canyon. "Maybe he did go up there to kill himself," she said, her back to Jackson.

"Hayes will find out why they think he was murdered. In the meantime—"

All the ramifications of this news hit her like a battering ram. "What happens if I'm dead?" She had been looking out into the darkness, but now swung her gaze on him. "Who inherits the money?"

"Natalie. The money would be used for her care until she was twenty-one, at which time her guardian—"

"Her *guardian?*"

"Nick named a guardian in case of your…death or incarceration."

Allie's voice broke. *"Who?"*

"Originally Drew was listed as guardian on the policies, but Nick changed that, too, right before he headed for the mountains." He met her gaze. "Megan, as your next closest kin, even though she isn't a blood relative."

She staggered under the weight of it. She couldn't deal with this now. She had the wedding. "The fireworks show is about to start," she said. "I have to finish—"

"I'm sure Dana will see that the rest of the wedding goes off like it is supposed to," Jackson said, blocking her escape. "No one expects you to continue, given what's happened."

"I took the job. I want to finish it," Allie said, hugging herself against the evening chill. "I thought you would understand that."

"I do. But—" His cell phone rang. "It's Hayes." He took the call.

She had no choice but to wait. She had to know what he'd found out at the police station. As she waited, she watched the lights of Big Sky glitter in the growing darkness that fell over the canyon. A breeze seemed to grow in the shadowed pines. The boughs began to move as if with the music still playing down in the barn.

After a moment, Jackson thanked his brother and disconnected. She remained looking off into the distance, her back to him, as he said, "Nick Taylor's remains were found in a shallow grave. There was a .45 bullet lodged in his skull. The trajectory of the bullet based on where it entered and exited, along with the fact that it appears someone tried to hide the body… It's being investigated as a homicide."

She felt a jolt when he mentioned that the bullet was a .45 caliber and knew Jackson would have seen it. Still, she didn't turn.

"Megan told me you bought a gun and that it disappeared from the cabin," he said. She could feel his gaze on her, burning into her back. He thought he knew her. She could imagine what was going through his mind. He would desperately want to believe she had nothing to do with her husband's murder. "Was the gun you purchased a—"

"Forty-five?" She nodded as she turned to look at him. "Everyone will believe I killed him. You're not even sure anymore, are you?"

"Allie—" He took a step toward her, but she held up her hand to ward him off. It had grown dark enough that she couldn't make out his expression unless he came closer, which was a godsend. She couldn't bear to see the disappointment in his face.

Below them on the mountain everyone was coming out of the barn to gather in the meadow for the fireworks. She suddenly ached to see her daughter. Natalie had been all that had kept her sane for so long. Right now, she desperately needed to hold her.

What would happen to Natalie now? She was trembling with fear at the thought that came to her and would no doubt have already come to the police—and eventually Jackson. She didn't want to be around when that happened.

"With my husband dead, that is three insurance policies for more than a million and a half," she said. "Mother Taylor is convinced I've made up all the stories about someone gaslighting me, as you call it. She thinks I have some plot to make myself rich at her poor Nicky's expense. I'm sure she's shared all of that with the police by now. Maybe I did do it."

He stepped to her and took her shoulders in his hands.

"Don't. You didn't kill your husband and you *know* damned well that I believe you."

"Your ex-wife, she was a liar and con woman, right? Isn't that why you were so afraid to get involved with me? What makes you so sure I'm not just like her?"

"You can't push me away." He lifted her chin with his fingers so she couldn't avoid his gaze. Their faces were only a few inches apart. "You aren't like her."

"What if I'm crazy?" Her voice broke. "Crazy like a fox?" The first of the fireworks exploded, showering down a glittering red, white and blue light on the meadow below them. The boom echoed in her chest as another exploded to the oos and ahs of the wedding party. She felt scalding tears burn her throat. "What if Mother Taylor is right and all of this is some subconscious plot I have to not only free myself of Nick, but walk away with a million and a half dollars, as well?"

JACKSON COULDN'T BEAR to see Allie like this. He pulled her to him and, dropping his mouth to hers, kissed her. She leaned into him, letting him draw her even closer as the kiss deepened. Fireworks lit the night, booming in a blaze of glittering light before going dark again.

Desire ignited his blood. He wanted Allie like he'd never wanted anyone or anything before. She melted into him, warm and lush in his arms, a moan escaping her lips.

Then suddenly he felt her stiffen. She broke away. "I can't keep doing this," she cried and, tearing herself from his arms, took off down the steps and through the trees toward the barn.

He started after her, but a voice from the darkness stopped him.

"Let her go."

He turned to find his brother Laramie standing in the

nearby trees. More fireworks exploded below them. "What are you doing, little brother?"

"I'm in love with her." The words were out, more honest than he'd been with even himself—let alone Allie.

"Is that right?" Laramie moved to him in a burst of booming light from the meadow below. "So what are you going to do about it?"

Jackson shook his head. "I…I haven't gotten that far yet."

"Oh, I think you've gotten quite far already." Laramie sighed. "I don't want to see you jump into anything. Not again."

"She is nothing like Juliet."

His brother raised a brow. "I knew one day you would fall in love again. It was bound to happen, but Jackson, this is too fast. This woman has too many problems. Hayes and I just came from the police station. They are going to be questioning her about her husband's murder. It doesn't look good."

"She had nothing to do with his death."

"She owns a .45 pistol, the one they suspect is the murder weapon."

Jackson sighed and looked toward the meadow below. It was cast in darkness. Had the fireworks show already ended? "She did but whoever is trying to have her committed, took it to set her up. You know as well as I do that someone has been gaslighting her."

Laramie shook his head. "We only know what Allie has been telling you."

His first instinct was to get angry with his brother, but he understood what Laramie was saying. There was no proof. Instead, the evidence against her was stacking up.

"I believe her and I'm going to help her," he said as he stepped past his brother.

"I just hope you aren't making a mistake," Laramie said behind him as Jackson started down the mountainside.

He'd only taken a few steps when he saw people running all over and heard Allie screaming Natalie's name. He took off running toward her.

"What's wrong?" he demanded when he reached her.

"Nat's gone!" Allie cried.

Chapter Fourteen

"She *can't* be gone," Jackson said. "She was with Dana, right?"

"Dana said the kids were all together, but after one of the fireworks went off, she looked over and Nat wasn't with them. She asked Hank and he said she spilled her lemonade on her dress and went to the bathroom to try to wash it off. Dana ran up to the house and the barn, but she wasn't there." Allie began to cry. "She found this, though." She held up the tie that had been on Nat's dress. "Natalie might have gone looking for me. Or someone took her—"

"Allie," he said, taking her shoulders in his hands. "Even if she left the meadow to go to the house, she couldn't have gotten far. We'll find her."

The search of the ranch area began quickly with everyone from the wedding party out looking for the child.

"I turned my back for just a moment," Dana said, sounding as distraught as Allie when Jackson caught up with her.

"It's not your fault. If anyone is to blame, it's me. I've been trying to help Allie and have only made things worse. I need to know something," he said as he watched the searchers coming off the mountain from the cabins. No Natalie. "Did you see anyone go toward the house about the time you realized she was gone?"

She shook her head. "You mean Drew or his mother? They both left earlier to go talk to the police."

"What about his sister, Sarah? Have you seen her?"

Dana frowned. "She didn't leave with them, now that I think about it, and I haven't seen her since Nat went missing."

Jackson spotted Belinda trying to comfort Allie down by the main house. "How about Megan?"

She shook her head. "I haven't seen either of them." Dana looked worried. "You don't think—"

He did think. He ran down the slope toward the house and Allie. "Did either of you see Sarah or Megan?"

They looked at him in surprise.

"They left together not long after the fireworks started," Belinda said. "Sarah said she had a headache and asked Megan to give her a ride."

Jackson looked at Allie. "You know where Sarah lives, right?"

"You think they took Nat?" Allie looked even more frightened.

"Belinda, stay here and keep us informed if the searchers find Nat. Come on. Let's see if they have Natalie or might have seen her since they left about the time she went missing."

EACH BREATH WAS a labor as Allie stared out the windshield into the darkness ahead. She fought not to break down but it took all of her strength. She'd never been so frightened or felt so helpless. All she could do was pray that Natalie was safe.

"If they took her, then I'm sure they wouldn't hurt her," she said, needing desperately to believe that. "Sarah might have thought it was getting too late for Natalie to be out. Or maybe Nat's dress was so wet—"

"We're going to find her." Jackson sounded convinced of that.

She glanced over at him. His strong hands gripped the

wheel as he drove too fast. He was as scared as she was, she realized. Like her, he must be blaming himself. If the two of them hadn't left the wedding…

"Tell me where to turn. I don't know where they live."

"Take a left at the Big Sky resort turnoff. Mother Taylor… Mildred lives up the mountain."

"They don't have that much of a head start," he said, sounding as if he was trying to reassure himself as much as her.

"This is all my fault." She didn't realize she'd said the words aloud until he spoke.

"No, if anyone is to blame it's me," he said as he reached over and squeezed her hand. "You have been going through so much and all I did was complicate things for you."

She let out a nervous laugh. "Are you kidding? I would have been in a straitjacket by now if it wasn't for you. I still might end up there, but at least I had this time when there was someone who believed me."

"I *still* believe you. You're not crazy. Nor did you have anything to do with your husband's death. You're being set up and, if it is the last thing I do, I'm going to prove it."

Allie couldn't help but smile over at him. "Thank you but I can't ask you to keep—"

"You're not asking. There's something else I need to say." He glanced over at her before making the turn at Big Sky then turned back to his driving. "I hadn't been with another woman since my ex. I didn't *want* anyone. The mere thought of getting involved again… Then I met you," he said shooting her a quick look as they raced up the mountain toward Big Sky Resort.

"Turn at the next left when we reach the top of the mountain," she said, not sure she wanted to hear what he had to say.

"I hadn't felt anything like that in so long and then we made love and…"

She really didn't need him to let her down easy. Not right now. All she wanted to think about was Natalie. If he was just doing this to keep her from worrying… "You don't have to explain."

"I do. I panicked because making love with you was so amazing and meant so much and…" He shook his head. "I…I just needed time to digest it all. And, truthfully, I was scared. Ford's mom did a number on me. Admittedly, we were both young, too young to get married, let alone have a child together. I had this crazy idea that we wanted the same things. Turned out she wanted money, a big house, a good time. When she got pregnant with Ford…" He slowed to make the turn.

"It's up this road about a mile. Turn left when you see the sign for Elk Ridge."

He nodded. "Juliet didn't want the baby. I talked her into having Ford. She hated me for it, said it was going to ruin her figure." He shook his head at the memory. "I thought that after he was born, her mothering instincts would kick in. My mistake. She resented him even more than she did me. She basically handed him to me and went out with her friends."

"I can't imagine."

He glanced over at her. "No, *you* can't." He sighed. "After that, she started staying out all night, wouldn't come home for days. Fortunately, the barbecue businesses took off like crazy so I could stay home with Ford. I asked for a divorce only to find out that my wife liked being a Cardwell and didn't want to give up what she had, which was basically no responsibilities, but lots of money and freedom to do whatever she wanted."

"Keep going up this road," she told him. Then after a moment, said, "She didn't want a divorce."

"No. She said that if I pushed it, she would take Ford."

"How horrible," Allie cried. Hadn't that been her fear

with Nick? Hadn't she worried that he would be a bastard and try to hurt them both when she told him she was leaving him?

"After the battle I fought to keep my son, I was…broken."

"I understand. The last thing you wanted was to get involved with a woman who only reminded you of what you'd been through."

He glanced over at her. "That was part of it." He didn't say more as he reached the turnoff for Mildred Taylor's house and the guesthouse where her daughter, Sarah, lived. He turned down it and Mildred's house came into view.

JACKSON HAD ALMOST told Allie how he felt about her. That he loved her. But as he'd turned and seen Mildred Taylor's big house, he'd realized the timing was all wrong. First they had to find Natalie.

He prayed she would be here, safe. But if so, did the Taylors seriously think they could get away with this? Had they told someone they were taking Natalie and the person just forgot or couldn't find Allie and left? Was there a logical explanation for this?

He hoped it was just a misunderstanding. But in his heart, he didn't believe for a minute that Allie had imagined the things that had been happening to her. Someone was behind this and they weren't finished with Allie yet. What scared him was that one of them could have murdered Nick.

His heart began to pound harder as he pulled in front of the large stone-and-log house set back against the mountainside. There were two vehicles parked in front and the lights were on inside the massive house. He parked and opened his door, anxious to put Nat in her mother's arms. Allie was out her door the moment he stopped.

"Who all lives here?" Jackson asked as he caught up to her.

"Just Mildred in the main house. Sarah stays in the guesthouse behind it. Drew lives down in Gateway but he stays with his mother a lot up here. That's his pickup parked next to Mildred's SUV so he must be here."

As Jackson passed Mildred's SUV, he touched the hood. Still warm. They at least hadn't been here long.

"What does Sarah drive?" he asked, glancing toward the dark guesthouse.

"A pearl-white SUV. I don't see it."

At Allie's knock, he heard movement inside the house. If they were trying to hide Natalie, it wouldn't do them any good. He looked back down the mountainside telling himself that if Natalie was in this house, he'd find her.

Drew opened the door and looked surprised to see them standing there.

"Where is Natalie?" Allie cried as she pushed past him.

"Natalie?" Drew barely got the word out before Jackson pushed past him, as well. The two of them stormed into the main part of the house.

Mildred was seated on one of the large leather couches facing the window in the living room, a glass of wine in her hand. She looked up in surprise.

"Where is she?" Allie demanded. "I know you have my daughter."

"Natalie?" Mildred asked, frowning. "You can't *find* her?"

"They seem to think we have her," Drew said, closing the front door and joining them. "We've been at the police station. Why would you think we had Natalie?"

"Allie, stay here. I'll search the house," Jackson said.

"You most certainly will not," Mildred cried. "I'll call the cops."

"Call the cops, but I suspect the marshal is already on his way here," he told her and wasn't surprised when Drew stepped in front of him as if to block his way.

"You really want to do this now? Your niece is missing.

If you don't have her, then we need to be out looking for her, not seeing who is tougher between you and me."

"We don't have her," Drew said, "and you're not—"

Jackson hit him and didn't wait around to see if he got up.

He stormed through the house, calling Nat's name. There were a lot of rooms, a lot of closets, a lot of places to look. But it didn't take him long to realize she wasn't here. Whatever they might have done with her, she wasn't in this house.

"I'm going to have you arrested for trespassing and barging into our house and attacking my son," Mildred threatened but hadn't made the call when he returned. Drew had a package of frozen peas he was holding to his eye as he came out of the kitchen.

"Mildred swears she hasn't seen Sarah," Allie told him.

"Well, Natalie isn't here. I think we should still check the guesthouse."

"You planning to break in?" Drew asked. "Or would you like me to get the key?"

Mildred pushed to her feet. "Drew, you are most certainly not going to—"

"Shut up, Mother," he snapped. "Aren't you listening? Natalie is missing. If I can help find her, I will. What I'd like to know is why you aren't upset about it. If you know where Nat is, Mother, you'd better tell me right now."

Jackson felt his cell phone vibrate, checked it and said, "I just got a text that the marshal is on his way. Mrs. Taylor, you could be looking at felony kidnapping," he warned.

ALLIE STARED AT HER mother-in-law, seeing a pathetic, lonely woman who now looked trapped.

"She's not in the guesthouse," Mildred said. "She's *fine*. She's with Sarah and Megan."

"Where?" Allie demanded, her heart breaking at the

thought of Megan being involved in this. "Why would they take her?"

Mildred met her gaze. "Because you're an unfit mother. Megan told me all about your mother and her family. Crazy, all of them. And you? You see things and do things that prove you can't raise my Nicky's baby girl. She needs *family.* Natalie needs her *grandmother,*" she said before bursting into tears.

"Call them and tell them to bring Natalie back," Jackson ordered.

"He's right, Mother. Natalie belongs with her mother."

"How can you say that?" Mildred cried, turning on her son. "I told you about all the crazy things she's been doing. Did you know she cut up all those lovely dresses my Nicky had bought her? She never liked them and with him gone—" Mildred stopped as if she felt Allie staring at her in shock. "She's *crazy.* Just look at her!"

"The dresses. I never told anyone other than Jackson about finding them cut up on my bed," Allie said, surprised by how normal her voice sounded. Even more surprised by the relief she felt. "It was the night Drew took Natalie and me to dinner. *You?* You bought the clothes in the closet that I found. No wonder you asked me about what I was wearing at the rehearsal dinner. You knew where I kept my checkbook in the desk drawer. Nick would have told you about the kind of clothes I liked. Forging my signature on a check wouldn't have been hard, not for a woman who has been forging her husband's signature on checks for years."

Mildred gasped. "Where would you get an idea like that?"

"*Your Nicky* told me. You've been stealing from the elderly man you married to keep up the lifestyle you believe you deserve. But you don't deserve my daughter."

"Is that true, Mother?" Drew asked with a groan.

"Never mind that cheap bastard. Men never stay so yes, I took advantage while it lasted and now he's divorcing me. Happy?" Mildred thrust her finger at Allie. "But you, you killed my Nicky!"

"How can you say that?" Allie demanded. "You can't really believe I followed him up into the mountains."

"You *paid* someone to kill him. I know you did," the older woman argued. "When I came over that weekend, you were packing up some of Nicky's belongings. You knew he was dead before we even heard."

"That was just some things he left out before he went hunting."

"She's lying," Mildred cried as she looked from Jackson to Drew. "She knew Nicky wasn't coming back. She was packing. I saw that she'd cleaned out the closet before she closed the bedroom door."

"I was packing my own things and Natalie's," Allie said. "I was planning to leave Nick. Ask Belinda. She'll tell you. I wanted a divorce."

Mildred looked shocked. "Why would you want to leave my Nicky? You must have found another man."

"No," Allie said, shaking her head. "I know how much you loved him but I didn't see the same man you did. Nick wasn't any happier than I was in the marriage."

"Oh, I have to sit down," Mildred cried. "Can't you see? She had every reason to want Nicky dead. She's admitted it."

"Make the call to your daughter, Mrs. Taylor," Jackson said, handing her his phone.

At the sound of a siren headed toward the house, Mildred took his phone.

"You'll get your daughter back, but only temporarily," her mother-in-law spat after making the call. "Once you go to prison for my Nicky's murder, you will get what you deserve and I will get my Nicky's baby."

"And all Nick's insurance money," Jackson said. "Isn't that what this is really about?"

Mildred didn't answer as Marshal Hud Savage pulled up out front.

Chapter Fifteen

Emotionally exhausted, all Allie could think about was holding her daughter. They'd all waited, the marshal included, until Megan and Sarah brought Natalie to the Taylor house.

Allie swept her daughter up into her arms, hugging her so tightly that Natalie cried, "Mama, you're squishing me!"

Hud took Mildred, Drew, Megan and Sarah down to the marshal's office to question them.

"Why don't you come stay at the ranch," Jackson suggested, but all Allie wanted to do was take her daughter home. "Okay, I'll drop you off there. I can give you a ride to the ranch in the morning to pick up your van."

She looked into his dark eyes and touched his arm. "Thank you."

They didn't talk on the drive to her cabin. Natalie fell asleep after complaining that she'd missed most of the fireworks. Apparently, Sarah and Megan had told her they were taking her to see her mama and that it was important.

As they drove, pockets of fireworks were going off around them. Allie had forgotten it was the Fourth of July. Even the wedding seemed like it had been a long time ago.

"If you need anything..." Jackson said after he'd insisted on carrying Natalie into her bed. He moved to the cabin door. "I'm here for you, Allie."

She could only nod, her emotions long spent.

"I'll see you tomorrow."

Allie doubted that. Jackson and Ford would be flying out. She told herself that she and Natalie were safe as she locked the front door, leaned against it and listened to Jackson drive away.

But in her heart she knew they wouldn't be safe until Nick's killer was caught.

"I RUINED TAG and Lily's wedding," Jackson said with a groan the next morning at breakfast.

"You did not," Dana said, patting his hand as she finished serving a huge ranch breakfast of elk steaks, biscuits and gravy, fried potatoes and eggs. She had invited them all down, saying that she knew it had been a rough night. Hud had left for his office first thing this morning.

The wedding couple had stayed at Big Sky Resort last night and flown out this morning to an undisclosed location for their two-week-long honeymoon.

"They loved everything about the wedding," Dana said. "They were just worried about Allie after Mildred's announcement and then concerned for Natalie. I'm just so thankful that she was found and is fine. I can't imagine what Sarah and Megan were thinking."

Jackson had filled everyone in on what had happened at the Taylors' and how apparently Mildred, Sarah and Megan had been gaslighting Allie.

"Oh, Allie must be heartbroken to find out her stepsister was in on it," Dana said.

"I'm sure Hud will sort it out," Jackson said as he watched his son eating breakfast with the Savage clan at the kid table. Ford, he noticed, had come out of his shell. Jackson couldn't believe the change in the boy from when they had arrived at the ranch. Montana had been good for his son.

"Natalie is safe and so is Allie, at least for the moment," he said. "The problem is Nick's murder," he said, dropping his voice, even though he doubted the kids could hear, given the amount of noise they were making at their table.

"They still don't know who killed him?" Dana asked.

Jackson shook his head. "Mildred is convinced Allie paid someone to do it. The police want to talk to her."

"You sound worried," Dana noted. "And your brothers haven't said a word," she said, looking from Hayes to Laramie and finally Jackson. "Why is that?"

"They've been helping me do some investigating," he admitted.

Dana rolled her eyes. "I should have known that was what was going on." She glanced at Hayes and Laramie. "You found something that makes her look guilty?"

"Someone is setting her up," Jackson said.

"The same people who tried to drive her crazy?" she asked.

"Maybe not. There could be more going on here than even we know." Jackson couldn't help sounding worried as he got to his feet. "Hayes and I are going to take her van to her. She called this morning. A homicide detective from Bozeman wants to see her."

ALLIE HAD AWAKENED in Natalie's bed to the sound of the phone. She'd expected it to be Jackson. That sent her heart lifting like helium. But as she reminded herself he was leaving today, her moment of euphoria evaporated.

Reaching for the receiver, she had a bad feeling it wasn't going to be good news. "We would like to ask you a few questions," the homicide detective told her. "When would be a good time?"

After she'd hung up, she'd called Jackson and told him the news.

"You knew this was coming. It's nothing to worry about," he'd told her, but she'd heard concern in his voice. "Do you want me to go with you?"

"No. This is something I have to do alone. Anyway, aren't you flying out today?"

Silence, then, "I canceled our flight."

"You shouldn't have done that," she said after a moment.

"Allie, I can't leave yet. I saw that the key is in the van. Hayes and I will bring it over."

"There is no hurry. I don't see the homicide detective until later."

Their conversation had felt awkward and ended just as badly. Allie told herself she couldn't keep leaning on Jackson. She knew now what Mildred and her daughter and Megan had done to her. She could understand Sarah going along with whatever her mother said, but Megan?

She'd felt like family. But then so had Drew.

Allie made Natalie her favorite pancakes when she woke up, then they went for a walk down by the river. Nat did love to throw rocks into the water. Allie watched the ripples they made, thinking about Jackson and the ripples he'd made in her life.

After a while, they walked back to the cabin. Dana had called saying she would love to take Natalie while Allie went to talk to the detective.

"If you trust me with her. I wouldn't blame you if you didn't. Just let me know."

Allie called Dana right back. "I would always trust you with Natalie and she would love to see the kids, not to mention Sugar, the horse."

Dana laughed and Allie could hear tears in her voice. "I was afraid you would never forgive me."

"There is nothing to forgive. Megan and Sarah took advantage of the fireworks show and the wedding."

"What were they thinking? Did they really believe they could get away with keeping her?"

"I suppose they thought I would come unglued, which

I did, proving that I was unbalanced. If it hadn't been for Jackson…" She really hadn't meant to go there.

"Is Natalie all right?"

"She didn't even realize anything was amiss. Apparently, they told her they were taking her to me, but when they reached Megan's motel room, they told her I was going to meet them there. Nat ended up falling asleep. So she had no idea what was going on."

"Thank goodness."

"I'll drop Nat off on my way, if that's okay."

"That's wonderful. We can't wait to see her. Tell her to wear her boots. We'll go for a ride."

"You NEED TO take the hint," Hayes said as he and Jackson drove away from Allie's cabin. They'd dropped off the van, Allie had thanked them and that was that, so Jackson knew what his brother was getting at. "Allie is handling all of this fine. I'm not sure there is anything you can do from here on out."

"You think she had him killed?" Jackson demanded.

Hayes shrugged. "I don't know her as well as you think you do. I don't think she paid anyone to do it. But if she gave Drew any kind of opening with her, I think he would have killed his brother for her—and the insurance money."

"She wasn't in cahoots with Drew. And stop doing that," he snapped as his brother shrugged again. "Do you realize how cynical you've become? Worse, does McKenzie?"

Hayes smiled. "Speaking of McKenzie… I'm opening a private investigator business here."

"You think that's a newsflash?" Jackson laughed. "We've all seen that coming for a mile. So when is the wedding?"

"I'm thinking we might elope. I'm not sure the family can live through another Cardwell Ranch wedding."

"Which reminds me, still no word from Austin?"

"You know our brother when he's on a case. But I am a little worried about him. I really thought he'd make Tag's wedding."

"Yeah, me too. Maybe I'll give a call down there. Knowing him, he probably didn't list any of us as emergency contacts."

ALLIE TRIED TO get comfortable in the chair the homicide detectives offered her. The room was like any office, no bare lightbulb shining into her eyes, no cops threatening her. But she still shifted in her chair.

On the drive here, she'd tried to concentrate on who might have killed Nick. Belinda had been up that trail with Nick when the two of them had been dating. Drew usually went hunting with his brother. Had Drew gone this time, as well, gotten in an argument with Nick and killed him?

She shuddered at the path her thoughts had taken. Did she really think someone in Nick's own family had killed him?

Better that than to think that her stepsister, Megan, had. Allie felt sick at the thought. Her sister had called this morning but Allie hadn't picked up.

"I need to explain," Megan had said on voice mail. "I did what I did for Natalie's sake. I love you and my niece. I really believed I was protecting you both. I had no idea Mildred and Sarah were doing those things to you, making you behave the way they told me you were. Please call me so we can talk about this."

The larger of the two homicide detectives cleared his voice. His name tag read Benson. "We need to know where you were the weekend your husband went up into the mountains."

"I was home that whole weekend."

"Did you talk to anyone? Anyone stop by?"

Allie tried to remember. Her mind was spinning. They

thought she'd had something to do with Nick's death? Of course they did, given the insurance policies and her mother-in-law's rantings and ravings.

Just yesterday, she'd been sure that Nick was alive. Jackson had been convinced, as well. She'd been even more convinced when she'd heard his voice at the séance. Nick's voice accusing her of killing him. She shivered at the memory.

"Mrs. Taylor?" the smaller of the two, whose name tag read Evans, asked.

She blinked. No one called her Mrs. Taylor. Mrs. Taylor was Nick's mother. "Please, call me Allie. I just need a moment to think." Had anyone stopped by that weekend?

Fighting all her conflicting thoughts, she tried to remember. Nick had left early, having packed the night before. He'd seemed excited about the prospect of going alone on this hunt. Why hadn't she noticed that something was wrong right there? It was the first red flag.

Had anyone stopped by? No. She frowned. She'd tried to call Belinda but hadn't been able to reach her, she recalled now. She'd wanted to tell her what Nick had said about making some changes when he returned from his hunting trip. She'd had misgivings about the trip even then and she'd needed to talk to someone. Had she worried that he might be thinking of killing himself?

"I don't remember anyone stopping by," she said, trying to keep her thoughts on the question. She ticked off everyone on her fingers. "I couldn't reach my friend Belinda." Had she tried Megan? "Or my stepsister, Megan. And my in-laws. I think that was the weekend that Mildred and Sarah went on a shopping trip to Billings. Drew… I don't know where he was. I didn't talk to him."

She looked up to see that both detectives were studying her. They were making her even more nervous.

"I was alone with my daughter that whole weekend." She

had no alibi. But they didn't really think she'd followed Nick up in the mountains and killed him, did they?

"Was it unusual for your husband to go hunting alone?"

"Very. I didn't think he had. I thought he was having an affair. I was surprised when I learned that he really had gone into the mountains."

The detectives shared a look before the lead one asked, "Did you have any reason to believe your husband was having an affair?"

"No. I guess it was wishful thinking. It would have made it easier for me."

The two shared another look. "Easier?"

She met the smaller detective's gaze. "I was going to leave Nick." Why not admit it? They probably already knew this after talking to her in-laws and Belinda and Megan. "But I didn't want him dead. You asked what I was doing that weekend? I didn't leave the house. I had my five-year-old daughter to take care of that weekend and I was busy packing."

"When were you planning to tell him?" Benson asked.

"As soon as he returned."

Evans picked up a sheet of paper from the desk. "Mrs. Tay— Excuse me, Allie, you own a .45 pistol?"

Chapter Sixteen

The gun. What had she been thinking when she'd bought it? Had she really thought that pulling it on Nick would be a good idea? She'd wanted something to protect herself for when she told him she was leaving.

Now she saw how ridiculous that was. Nick would have taken it away from her, knowing she couldn't shoot him and then he would have been so furious....

"Yes, I bought the gun for protection."

Benson raised a brow. "Protection? Against whom?"

"I was planning to leave my husband. My daughter and I would be alone—"

"But you hadn't left him yet," Evans pointed out. "So why buy a .45 pistol only days before your husband was to go on his hunting trip?"

"I…I…was afraid of how Nick was going to take it when he returned and I told him I was leaving him. Sometimes he scares me."

The two detectives exchanged another look.

"But it was impulsive and silly because Nick would have known I couldn't use it on him. He would have taken it away from me and…" She swallowed.

"You were afraid of your husband," Benson said.

"Sometimes."

"Where is the gun now?" Evans asked.

"I don't know. When I heard that Nick had been killed

with a .45, I looked for it, but it was gone." Allie could see the disbelief written all over their faces. Hadn't she known when she looked that it would be gone?

"I think someone is trying to set me up for his murder," she blurted out and instantly regretted it when she saw their expressions. Apparently, they'd heard this type of defense before.

"You're saying someone took the gun to frame you?" Benson asked. "Who knew you'd bought it?"

Allie met his gaze. "I didn't tell anyone, if that is what you're asking."

"Who had access to your house?" Evans asked.

"It's an old cabin. I don't know how many people might have a key. Nick was always going to change the locks…"

"Your in-laws? Did they have keys?" Benson asked.

"Yes."

"Friends?"

"Belinda and my stepsister, Megan, know where there's a key to get in."

"Where did you keep the gun that someone could have found it? You have a five-year-old. I assume you didn't just leave the gun lying around," Benson asked.

"Of course not. I put it on the top shelf of the closet. It wasn't loaded."

"But there were cartridges for it with the gun?"

She nodded.

"When was the last time you saw it?" Evans asked.

"The day I bought it. I put it on the shelf behind some shoe boxes… I'd forgotten all about it with Nick's…death… and all."

"So you were just going to leave him," Evans said. "This man who you said scared you sometimes, you were going to allow him to have joint custody of your child?"

"It hadn't gotten that far. I guess it would have been up to the court—"

"Oh, so you'd already seen a lawyer about a divorce?" Benson asked.

"Not yet. I couldn't afford to see one until I got a job and Nick wouldn't allow me to work."

The detectives exchanged looks.

"Was your husband abusive?" Benson asked not unkindly.

Allie hesitated. "He was…controlling."

"And he scared you," Evans said.

"Yes, sometimes. What is it you want me to say? He wasn't a good husband or father to our daughter. And yes, sometimes he scared me."

"Mrs. Taylor, did you kill your husband?" Evans asked.

"No. I told you. I could never—"

"Did you get your brother-in-law, Drew, or someone else close to you to do the killing for you?" Benson asked.

"*No!* I didn't want to be married to Nick anymore but I didn't want him dead."

Evans leaned forward. "But look how it turned out. Nick is no longer around to scare you, even sometimes. Your daughter is safe from him. And you are a wealthy woman thanks to his insurance money. Better than a divorce and a lengthy battle over your daughter, wouldn't you say?"

Allie felt as if the detectives had beaten her as she stumbled out of the police station. For a moment she forgot where she'd parked the van. Panic sent her blood pressure soaring before she spotted it. There it was, right where she'd left it. And there was…

"Jackson?"

He pushed off the van and moved quickly to her. "I had to see you before I left."

She frowned, still feeling off balance. "I thought you weren't flying out yet?"

"It's my brother Austin. He's a sheriff's deputy in Texas. He's been shot. He's critical. I have to fly out now. Franklin and Mom already left. Hayes, Laramie and I are taking the corporate jet as soon as I get to the airport."

"I'm so sorry, Jackson. Does Tag know?"

"We weren't able to reach him. He and Lily wanted their honeymoon to be a secret… Ford is staying with Dana until I get back. But I couldn't leave without seeing you. Are you all right?"

She started to say she was fine, but she couldn't get the lie past her lips. Her eyes filled with tears. "They think I killed Nick. Everyone does."

"Not me," he said and pulled her into his arms. "When I get back, we'll sort this out. I'm sorry I have to go."

She pulled back, brushed at her tears. "I'll say a prayer for your brother." As he ran to his rented SUV, she turned in time to see Detective Evans watching her from the front of the building. He looked like a man who'd just received a gift he hadn't expected. Jackson Cardwell. Another motive as to why she'd want her husband gone for good.

THE JET OWNED by the corporation was waiting on the tarmac when Jackson arrived at the airport. He ran to climb aboard and Laramie alerted the captain that they were ready.

"Have you heard any more from Mom or the hospital?" Jackson asked as he buckled up.

"I just got off the phone with Mom," Hayes said. "Austin's still in surgery." His tone was sufficient for Jackson to know it didn't look good.

"Do we know what happened?" he asked as the plane began to taxi out to the runway.

"You know how hard it is to get anything out of the sheriff's department down there," Hayes said. "But I got the impression he was on one of the dangerous cases he seems to like so well." He raked a hand through his hair. "There was a woman involved. He'd apparently gone into a drug cartel to get her out."

"That sounds just like Austin," Jackson said with a sigh as the jet engine roared and the plane began to race down the runway. "Did he get her out?"

"Don't know. Doubtful, though, since some illegal immigrants found him after he'd been shot and got him to a gas station near the border."

Hayes shook his head. "Some of the same illegal immigrants his department is trying to catch and send back over the border. What a mess down there. I'm glad I'm done with it."

His brothers looked at him in surprise as the plane lifted off the ground.

"McKenzie and I signed the papers on a ranch in the canyon not far from Cardwell Ranch. When I get back, we're eloping. She's already looking for some office space for me at Big Sky to open a private investigation office up here."

"Congratulations," Laramie said.

"Have you told Mom?" Jackson asked. "I'm wondering how she is going to feel losing another son to Montana?" The plane fell silent as he realized she might be losing another son at this very moment, one that not even Montana got a chance to claim.

Speaking of Montana, he thought as he looked out the window at the mountains below them. He'd hated leaving Allie, especially as upset as she'd been. He promised himself he would return to the canyon just as soon as he knew his brother was going to be all right.

He said a prayer for Austin and one for Allie, as well.

DANA HAD CALLED to say she was taking the kids on a horseback ride and that Allie could pick Natalie up later, if that was all right. Ford apparently was very upset and worried about his uncle Austin, so Dana was trying to take their minds off everything for a while.

Not wanting to go back to an empty cabin, Allie had

busied herself with errands she'd put off since the wedding preparation. It was late afternoon by the time she got home. She'd called the ranch only to find out that Dana and the kids had gone to get ice cream and would be back soon.

Allie was carrying in groceries and her other purchases when she heard the vehicle pull up. She'd hoped to get everything put away before she went to pick up Natalie. She carried the bags into the cabin, dumping them on the kitchen counter, before she glanced out the window to see her mother-and sister-in-law pull up. She groaned as the two got out and came to the door.

For just an instant, she thought about not answering their knock, but they must have seen her carrying in her groceries. Mildred wasn't one to take the hint and go away.

"I just got back from the police station," she said as she opened the door. "I'm really not in the mood for visitors." She couldn't believe either of them would have the gall to show their faces around here after what they'd done. Well, they weren't coming in. Whatever they had to say, they could say it on the front step.

Allie had already talked to Hud this morning. He'd questioned all of them last night, but had had to let them all go. Maybe they had come by to apologize, but Allie doubted it.

"I just got a call from the police," Mildred said indignantly. "Why would you tell them that Sarah and I went to Billings the weekend my Nicky was killed?"

"I thought you had." She knew she shouldn't have been surprised. No apology for what they had tried to do to her.

"We'd planned to go, but Sarah was sick that whole weekend." She sniffed. "I was alone when I got the call about my Nicky." She glared at her daughter for a moment. "Sarah had taken my car down to the drugstore to get more medicine since her car was in the shop. I couldn't even leave the house to go to Drew." Mildred sighed.

"I'm sorry you were alone, Mother. I came right back. I

couldn't have been gone more than five minutes after you got the call," Sarah said.

"That was the longest five minutes of my life," Mildred said with another sniff.

"I guess I had forgotten the two of you hadn't gone to Billings, but I'm sure you straightened it out with the police," Allie said. "And Sarah couldn't have known that would be the time you would get the call about Nick," Allie pointed out.

Sarah gave her a grateful smile, then added, "I hate to ask, but do you happen to have a cola in your fridge?"

"Oh, for crying out loud, Sarah, how many times have I told you that stuff is horrible for you?" her mother demanded.

"Help yourself," Allie said, moving to the side of the doorway to let her pass. She saw that the sun had disappeared behind Lone Mountain, casting the canyon in a cool darkness. Where had this day gone? "I hate to run you off, but I have to go pick up Natalie."

"Once this foolishness is over, I hope you'll forgive me and let me spend some time with my granddaughter," Mildred said.

As Sarah came out with a can of cola, Allie moved aside again to let her pass, hoping they would now leave.

Mildred looked in the yard at Nick's pickup, where it had been parked since someone from the forest service had found it at the trailhead and had it dropped off. "Why are you driving that awful van of yours? You should either drive Nicky's pickup or sell it. Terrible waste to just let it sit."

Allie planned to sell the pickup but she'd been waiting, hoping in time Mildred wouldn't get so upset about it.

"I'd like to buy it," Sarah said, making them both turn to look at her in surprise.

"What in the world do you need with Nicky's pickup?"

Mildred demanded. "I'm not giving you the money for it and I couldn't bear looking at it every day."

"It was just a thought," Sarah said as she started toward her SUV. The young woman took so much grief from her mother.

Her gaze went to Nick's pickup. The keys were probably still in it, she realized. As Sarah climbed behind the wheel and waited for her mother to get into the passenger side of the SUV, Allie walked out to the pickup, opened the door and reached inside to pull the keys.

The pickup smelled like Nick's aftershave and made her a little sick to her stomach. She pocketed the keys as she hurriedly closed the door. The truck was Nick's baby. He loved it more than he did either her or Natalie. That's why she was surprised as she started to step away to see that the right rear panel near the back was dented. She moved to the dent and ran her fingers over it. That would have to be fixed before she could sell it since the rest of the truck was in mint condition.

Just something else to take care of, she thought as she dusted what looked like chalky white flakes off her fingers. She looked up and saw that her in-laws hadn't left. Mildred was going on about something. Sarah was bent toward the passenger seat apparently helping her mother buckle up. Mildred was probably giving her hell, Allie thought.

When Sarah straightened, she looked up from behind the wheel and seemed surprised to see Allie standing by Nick's truck. Her surprise gave way to sadness as she looked past Allie to her brother's pickup.

Was it possible Sarah really did want Nick's pickup for sentimental reasons? Maybe she should have it. Allie had never thought Sarah and her brother were that close. Well, at least Nick hadn't been that crazy about his sister. He'd been even more disparaging than his mother toward Sarah.

Allie met her sister-in-law's dark gaze for a moment,

feeling again sorry for her. Maybe she would just give her the pickup. She waved as Sarah began to pull away, relieved they were finally leaving.

Her cell phone rang. She hoped it was Jackson with news of his brother. She said a silent prayer for Austin before she saw that it was Dana.

"Is everything all right?" Allie asked, instantly afraid.

"Ford is still upset about his uncle. Natalie told him that you were picking her up soon…"

Allie knew what was coming. She couldn't bear the thought. She wanted Natalie home with her. The way things were going, she feared she might soon be under arrest for Nick's murder. She didn't know how much time she and Nat had together.

"Natalie wishes to speak with you," Dana said before Allie could say no.

"Mama?" Just the sound of her daughter's voice made her smile. "Please say I can stay. Ford is very sad about his uncle. Please let me stay."

"Maybe Ford could come stay with you—"

"We're all going to sleep in the living room in front of the fire. Mrs. Savage said we could. She is going to make popcorn. It is Mary and Hank's favorite."

Allie closed her eyes, picturing how perfect it would be in front of Dana's fireplace in that big living room with the smell of popcorn and the sound of children's laughter. She wanted to sleep right in the middle of all of them.

"Of course you need to stay for your new friend," she heard herself say as tears burned her eyes. "Tell Mrs. Savage that I will pick you up first thing in the morning. I love you."

"I love you, too, Mama." And Natalie was gone, the phone passed to Dana who said, "I'm sorry. This was the kids' idea."

"It's fine."

"What about you? How did it go with the police?"

"As expected. They think I killed Nick. Or at least got someone to do it for me."

"That's ridiculous. Allie, listen, you shouldn't be alone. Why don't you come stay here tonight? I think you need your daughter. Do you like butter on your popcorn? Come whenever you want. Or take a little time for yourself. If you're like me, when was the last time you got a nice leisurely bath without being interrupted? Whatever you need, but bring your pjs. We're having a pajama party. Right now the kids all want to go help feed the animals. See you later."

AS THE JET touched down just outside of Houston, Hayes got the call from their mother. Jackson watched his expression, waiting for the news. Relief flooded his brother's face. He gave thumbs up and disconnected.

"Mom says Austin is out of surgery. The doctor says he should make it."

Jackson let out the breath he'd been holding. As the plane taxied toward the private plan terminal, he put in a call to Allie. It went straight to voice mail.

He left a message, telling her the good news, then asking her to call when she got the message. "I'm worried about you." As he disconnected, he realized he'd been worried the entire flight about both his brother and Allie.

"I can't reach Allie."

His brothers looked at him in concern as the plane neared the small brightly lit terminal. It was already dark here, but it would still be light in Montana.

"Call Dana," Hayes said. "She's probably over there."

He called. "No answer."

"They probably went for a horseback ride," Laramie said. "Wasn't that what Ford told you they were going to do the last time you talked to him?"

Jackson nodded, telling himself his brother was probably

right. He glanced at Hayes. He understood what Laramie couldn't really grasp. Laramie was a businessman. Hayes was a former sheriff's deputy, a private investigation. He understood Jackson's concern. There was a killer still loose in Montana.

The plane came to a stop. Jackson tried Allie again. The call again went straight to voice mail. He got Mildred Taylor's number and called her.

"Have you seen Allie?" he asked. He couldn't explain his fear, just a feeling in the pit of his stomach that was growing with each passing minute.

"Earlier. She wouldn't even let me in her house." She sniffed. "She was on her way to Cardwell Ranch to pick up Natalie the last I saw of her. Driving that old van. Why she doesn't drive Nickie's pickup I will never—"

He disconnected and tried Dana. Still no answer. He tried Allie again. Then he called the marshal's office in Big Sky.

"Marshal Savage is unavailable," the dispatcher told him.

"Is there anyone there who can do a welfare check?"

"Not at the moment. Do you want me to have the marshal call you when he comes in?"

Jackson started to give the dispatcher his number but Hayes stopped him.

"Take the plane," Hayes said. "Mother said it would be hours before we could even see Austin. I'll keep you informed of his progress."

"Are you kidding?" Laramie demanded. "What is it with you and this woman? Have you forgotten that she's the number one suspect in her husband's murder?"

"She didn't kill him," Jackson and Hayes said in unison.

"Let us know as soon as you hear something," Hayes said.

Jackson hugged his brother, relieved that he understood. He moved to cockpit and asked the pilot how long before they could get the plane back in the air. As Hayes and Laramie disembarked, he sat down again and buckled his seatbelt, trying to remain calm.

He had no reason to believe anything had happened. And yet…that bad feeling he'd gotten when her phone had gone to voice mail had only increased with each passing second. His every instinct told him that Allie was in real trouble.

Chapter Seventeen

Allie had taken a hot bath, but had kept it short. She was too anxious to see her daughter. She changed her clothes, relieved she was going to Dana's. She really didn't want to be alone tonight. She'd heard Natalie's happy chatter in the background and couldn't wait to reach the ranch.

In fact, she had started out the door when she realized she didn't have her purse or her van keys. Leaving the door open, she turned back remembering that she'd left them on the small table between the living room and kitchen when she brought in her groceries earlier.

She was sure she'd left her purse on the table, but it wasn't there. As she started to search for it, she began to have that awful feeling again. Her mind reeled. Mildred wasn't still fooling with her, was she? No Mildred hadn't come into the cabin. But Sarah had. Why would Sarah hide her purse? It made no sense.

Racking her brain, she moved through the small cabin. The purse wasn't anywhere. On her way back through, she realized she must have left it in the van. She was so used to leaving her purse on that small table, she'd thought she remembered doing it again.

She started toward the open door when a dark figure suddenly filled the doorway. The scream that rose in her throat came out a sharp cry before she could stop it.

"Drew, you scared me. I didn't hear you drive up."

"My truck's down the river a ways. I was fishing...."

The lie was so obvious that he didn't bother finishing it. He wasn't dressed for fishing nor was he carrying a rod.

"The truth is, I wanted to talk to you and after everything that's happened, I thought you'd chase me off before I could have my say."

"Drew, this isn't a good time. I was just leaving."

He laughed. "That's exactly why I didn't drive up in your yard. I figured you'd say something just like that."

"Well, in this case, it's true. Natalie is waiting for me. I'm staying at Cardwell Ranch tonight. Dana is going to be wondering where I am if I don't—"

"This won't take long." He took a breath. "I'm so sorry for everything."

Allie felt her blood heat to boiling. No one in this family ever listened to her. How dare he insist she hear him out when she just told him she was leaving? "You and your mother tried to drive me insane."

"I didn't know anything about that, I swear," Drew cried. "Mother told me that you had already forgotten about Nick. It was breaking her heart. She said you needed to be reminded and if you saw someone who looked like Nick..."

"You expect me to believe that?"

He shrugged. "It's true. I did it just to shut her up. You know how Mother is."

She did. She also knew arguing about this now was a waste of time and breath. She glanced at the clock on the mantel. "I really need to go."

"Just give me another minute, please. Also I wanted to apologize for the other night. I had too much to drink." He shook his head. "I don't know what I was thinking. But you have to know, I've always liked you." He looked at her shyly. "I would have done anything for you and now the cops think I killed Nick for you."

Her pulse jumped, her heart a thunder in her chest. "That's ridiculous."

"That's what I told them. I could never hurt my brother. I loved Nick. But I have to tell you, I was jealous of him when he married you."

"Drew, I really don't have time to get into this right—"

"Don't get me wrong," he said as if she hadn't spoken. "If I thought there was chance with you…"

A ripple of panic ran up her spine. "There isn't, Drew."

"Right. Jackson Cardwell."

"That isn't the reason."

"Right," he said sarcastically. His jaw tightened, his expression going dark. She'd been married to his brother long enough to know the signs. Nick could go from charming to furious and frightening in seconds. Apparently so could his brother.

"Drew—"

"What if I did kill him for you, Allie?" He stepped toward her. "What if I knew where he would be up that trail? What if I wanted to save you from him? You think I don't know how he was with you?" He let out a laugh. "Jackson Cardwell isn't the only knight in shining armor who wants to come to your rescue."

She didn't want to hear his confession and feared that was exactly what she was hearing. "Drew, I would never want you to hurt your brother for any reason, especially for me."

"Oh yea? But what if I did, Allie? Wouldn't you owe me something?"

He took another a step toward her.

She tried to hold her ground but Drew was much stronger, much larger, much scarier. With Nick, she'd learned that standing up to him only made things worse. But she was determined that this man wasn't going to touch her. She'd backed down too many times with Nick.

"This isn't happening, Drew." She stepped to the side

and picked up the poker from the fireplace. "It's time for you to go."

She could almost read his mind. He was pretty sure he could get the poker away from her before she did much bodily harm to him. She lifted it, ready to swing, when she heard a vehicle come into the yard.

Drew heard it to. "Jackson Cardwell to the rescue again?"

But it couldn't be Jackson. He was in Texas by now.

Allie was relieved to see his sister Sarah stick her head in the door. "I hope I'm not interrupting anything," she said into the tense silence.

"Not at all," Allie assured her sister-in-law. Her voice sounded more normal than she'd thought it would. Had Drew just confessed to killing Nick? "Drew was just leaving."

"We're not through talking about this," he said as he started for the door.

"Oh, I think we already covered the subject. Goodbye Drew."

"Is everything all right?" Sarah asked as Allie returned the poker to its spot next to the fireplace. She stepped in and closed the door behind her.

"Fine. You didn't happen to see my purse when you were here earlier, did you? Dana is expecting me and I can't seem to find it."

"No. You still haven't picked up Natalie?"

"No, Dana invited me for a sleepover with the kids. I was just heading there when Drew arrived."

"I didn't see his truck," Sarah said glancing toward the window.

"He said he parked it down river where he was fishing." She glanced around the living room one more time. "I need to find my purse and get going."

"Your purse? Oh, that explains why you didn't answer

your cell phone. I tried to call you," Sarah said. "Do you want me to help you look?"

"No, maybe I'll just take Nick's truck." The idea repulsed her, but she was anxious to get to the ranch. "I'm sure my purse will turn up. Oh, that's right, I was going out to check the van and see if I left it there when Drew showed up."

"So you're off to a kids sleepover?"

Allie knew she should be more upset with Sarah for taking Natalie last night, but Sarah had always done her mother's bidding. Allie couldn't help but feel sorry for the woman.

"Nat wanted to spend the night over there for Ford. He's upset about his uncle Austin who was shot down in Texas. His brothers should be at the hospital by now. No wonder I haven't heard anything with my cell phone missing."

"Natalie and Ford sure hit it off, didn't they? It's too bad Nat doesn't have a sibling. I always thought you and Nick would have another child."

Allie found Nick's truck keys in her jacket pocket and held them up. "If you still want Nick's truck, you can have it. I was planning to sell it. But the back side panel is dented." She frowned. "It's odd that Nick didn't mention it. You know how he was about truck…"

Her thoughts tumbled over each other in a matter of an instant as her gaze went to her fingers and she remembered the white flakes she'd brushed off the dent. It hadn't registered at the time. The dent. The white paint from the vehicle that had hit it. Pearl white on Nick's black pickup.

Nick would have been out of his mind if someone had hit his pickup. So it couldn't have happened before his hunting trip, which meant it happened where? At the trailhead?

ANOTHER VEHICLE MUST have hit the pickup. Allie's thoughts fell into a straight, heart-stopping line. A pearl-white vehicle like the one Sarah was having repaired the day the call came about Nick's death.

Allie felt the hair rise on the back of her neck as she looked up and saw Sarah's expression.

"I knew you would figure it out the minute I saw you standing next to the dent in Nick's pickup. Nick was so particular about his truck. One little scratch and he would have been losing his mind. Isn't that what you were realizing?"

"Oh Sarah," she said, her heart breaking.

"That's all you have to say to the woman who killed your husband?" she asked as she pulled Allie's .45 out of her pocket and pointed the barrel at Allie's heart.

JACKSON HAD LEFT his rental car at the Bozeman airport. The moment the jet landed he ran to it and headed up the canyon. He tried Allie again. Still no answer. He left a message just in case there was a good reason she wasn't taking calls.

The only reason he could come up with was that she was at Dana's with the kids and didn't want to be disturbed. But she would have taken his calls. She would have wanted to know how Austin was doing.

He tried Dana and was relieved when at least she answered. "I'm looking for Allie. Have you seen her?"

"Not yet. I talked to her earlier. I told her to take a nice hot, long bath and relax, then come over for a sleepover." He could hear Dana let out a surprised sound. "I didn't realize it was so late. She should have been here by now."

"Her calls are going straight to voice mail."

"I'm sure she's just running late..." Dana sounded worried. "How is Austin?"

"He's out of surgery. The doctor said he should make it. I left Hayes and Laramie in Houston."

"Where are you now?"

"On my way to Allie's cabin. If you hear from her, will you please call me?"

He disconnected and drove as fast as he could through the winding narrow canyon. Something was wrong. Dana felt it, too. He prayed that Allie was all right. But feared she wasn't.

Realizing his greatest fear, he called Drew's number. When he'd heard the part Allie's brother-in-law had played in gaslighting her, he'd wanted to punch Drew again. He didn't trust the man, sensed he was a lot like Nick had been; another reason to hate the bastard.

But Jackson also worried that Drew might have killed Nick. The problem was motive. He wouldn't benefit from his brother's death since Nick had changed his beneficiaries on his insurance policy. Or was there something else Drew wanted more than money?

It came to him in a flash. Allie. If he had her, he would also have Nick's money and Nick's life.

Drew answered on the third ring. "What?" He sounded drunk.

Jackson's pulse jumped. "Have you seen Allie?"

"Who the hell is this?"

"Jackson Cardwell." He heard Drew's sneer even on the phone.

"What do *you* want? Just call to rub it in? Well, you haven't got Allie yet so I wouldn't go counting your chickens—"

His heart was pounding like a war drum. "Is she with you?"

Drew laughed. "She's having a sleepover but not with me. Not yet."

"She isn't at the sleepover. When did you see her?"

Finally picking up on Jackson's concern, he said, "She was with my sister at the cabin."

Jackson frowned. "Your sister?"

"They both think I killed Nick. But Sarah had more of a motive than I do. She hated Nick, especially since he'd been trying to get Mother to kick her out. Sarah might look sweet, but I have a scar from when we were kids. She hit me with a tire iron. A tire iron! Can you believe that?"

Jackson saw the turnoff ahead. As he took it, his headlights flashed on the cabin down the road. There were three vehicles parked out front. Nick's black pickup. Allie's van. Sarah's pearl-white SUV.

Chapter Eighteen

"I don't understand," Allie said. "Why would you kill your brother?"

Sarah smiled. "Sweet, lovable *Nickie?* You of all people know what he was like. You had to know the way he talked about me."

Allie couldn't deny it. "He was cruel and insensitive, but—"

"He was trying to get Mother to kick me out without a cent!" Her face reddened with anger. "I gave up my life to take care of her and Nickie is in her ear telling her I am nothing but a parasite and that if she ever wants to see me get married, she has to kick me out and force me to make it on my own. Can you believe that?"

She could. Nick was often worried about any money that would be coming to him via his mother. He was afraid Sarah would get the lion's share because his mother felt sorry for her.

"He was jealous," Allie said. "He was afraid you were becoming her favorite just because she depends on you so much."

Sarah laughed. "Her *favorite?* She can't stand the sight of me. She'd marry me off in a heartbeat if she could find someone to take me off her hands."

"That isn't true. You know she would be lost without you." With a start, Allie realized that Mildred was going to get a chance to see what life was like without Sarah once Sarah went to prison. That is, unless she got away with murdering Nick. With Allie out of the way, Sarah just might.

"I still can't believe you killed him," Allie said as she searched her mind for anything within reach of where she was standing that she could use to defend herself. Something dawned on her. "How did you get my gun?"

"Mother had sent me to your cabin to see if you still had that pink sweater she gave you for Christmas. You never wore it and it was driving her crazy. I told her pink didn't look good on you, but she got it on sale… You know how she is."

Oh yes, she knew. That ugly pink sweater. Allie had put the gun under it behind the shoe boxes.

"When I found the gun, I took it. I was thinking I would try to scare Nick. After all, we have the same genes. He should have known I could be as heartless as him. But Nick had always underestimated me. I tried to talk to him, but he went off on women, you in particular."

Allie blinked in surprise. *"Me?"*

"He said some women needed to be kept in their place and that you thought you were going to leave him and take his child. He had news for you. He laughed, saying how you'd been stealing small amounts of his money thinking he wouldn't notice but he was on to you. He'd given you a few days to think about what you were doing, but when he came back there were going to be big changes. He was going to take you in hand. He said, 'I'll kill her before I'll let her leave me.' Then he told me to get out of his way and took off up the trail."

So Nick hadn't been promising to change, she thought. He was going to change her when he got back. Allie felt sick to her stomach, imagining what Nick would have been like if he had ever returned home to find her packing to leave him.

"His parting shot was to yell back at me. 'You big fat ugly pig. Go home to your mommy because when I get back your butt is out of that guesthouse.' Then he laughed and disappeared into the trees."

"Oh, Sarah, I'm so sorry. Nick was horrible. If you tell the police all of this—and I will back you up—I'm sure they will—"

"Will what? Let me go? You can't be that naive. I'll go to prison."

Allie had a crazy thought that prison would be preferable to living with Mildred Taylor.

"No, Allie, there is another way. You are the only one who knows what I did."

"If you kill me, they'll eventually catch you and since this will be cold-blooded murder, you will never get out of prison. Don't throw your life away because of Nick."

"I'm going to make you a deal," Sarah said. "I will spare your daughter if you do what I say."

"What? You would hurt Natalie?" Allie's terror ramped up as she realized this was a woman who felt no remorse for killing her own brother. Nor would she feel any for killing her sister-in-law now. That she could even think of hurting Natalie...

"Do you know why I look like I do?" Sarah asked. "I made myself fat after my mother's first divorce when I was just a little older than Natalie." She stepped closer, making Allie take a step back. "My stepfather thought I was adorable and couldn't keep his hands off me. My other stepfathers were just as bad until I gained enough weight that, like my mother, they only had contempt for me."

Allie couldn't hold back the tears. "I'm so sorry. I had no idea."

"No one did. My mother knew, though." Her eyebrow

shot up. "That surprises you?" She laughed. "You really have no idea what *Mother Taylor* is capable of doing or why she dotes on her granddaughter. This latest husband is divorcing her, but there will be another husband, one who will think your little Natalie is adorable. Think about that. You do what I say and I will make sure what happened to me doesn't happen to Nat."

Allie was too stunned almost to breathe. What was Sarah saying?

"That's right, Mother Taylor *needs* Natalie," her sister-in-law said. "Now you can either take this gun and shoot yourself or I will shoot you. But if I have to do it, I will probably get caught as you say and go to prison. Imagine what will happen to Natalie without me here to protect her. Oh, and don't even think about turning the gun on me because trust me I will take you with me and Natalie will have a new grandpa, one who will adore her."

Allie couldn't bear the choice Sarah was demanding she make. "Natalie needs me," she pleaded as she looked at the .45 her sister-in-law held out to her.

"She needs me more. Just imagine the danger Natalie would have been in if I hadn't warned you."

"Don't you think I suspected something was wrong at that house? I didn't like Natalie going there. I didn't trust your family."

"With good reason as it turns out. You have good mothering instincts. I wonder what my life would have been like if I'd had a good mother?"

Allie's heart went out to her even though the woman was determined she would die tonight. "I'm so sorry. Sarah, but we don't have to do this. I won't tell the police about the dent in the pickup."

"You're too honest. Every time you saw me, we would both know." She shook her head. "One day you would have to clear your conscience. You know what would happen to me if I went to prison. No, this is the best way. Think of your daughter."

How could she think of anything else? That's when she heard the vehicle approaching.

Sarah got a strange look on her face as she cocked her head at the sound of the motor roaring up into the yard. "This has to end now," she said.

Allie couldn't imagine who had just driven up. Dana and the kids? She couldn't take the chance that someone else would walk into this.

She grabbed for the gun.

JACKSON HIT THE door running. He told himself he was going to look like a damned fool barging in like this. But all his instincts told him something was very wrong.

As he burst through the door, he saw Allie and Sarah. Then he saw the gun they were struggling over.

The sound of the report in the tiny cabin was deafening. Jackson jumped between them going for the gun that Sarah still gripped in her hands. The silence after the gunshot was shattered as Allie began to scream.

Jackson fought to get the gun out of Sarah's hands. She was stronger than she looked. Her eyes were wide. She smiled at him as she managed to pull the trigger a second time.

The second silence after the gunshot was much louder.

"Allie, are you hit?" Jackson cried as he wrenched the gun from Sarah's hand.

She looked at him, tears in her eyes, and shook her head.

For a moment all three of them stood there, then Sarah fell to her knees, Allie dropping to the floor with her, to take the woman in her arms.

"She killed herself," Allie said to Jackson. "She could have killed me, but she turned the gun on herself." Still holding Sarah, Allie began to cry.

Jackson pulled out the phone, tapped in 911 and asked for an ambulance and the marshal, but one look at Sarah and he also asked for the coroner.

Epilogue

Be careful who you marry—including the family you marry into. That had been Jackson's mother's advice when he'd married Juliet. He hadn't listened. But Allie's in-laws made Juliet's look like a dream family.

"If you want to file charges," Marshal Hud Savage was saying. "You can get your mother-in-law for trespassing, vandalism, criminal mischief…but as far as the gaslighting…"

"I don't want to file charges," Allie said. "The real harm she's done… Well, there isn't a law against it, at least not for Mildred. And like you said, no way to prove it. How is Mildred?"

After what Allie had told him, Jackson hoped the woman was going through her own private hell. She deserved much worse.

"She's shocked, devastated, but knowing Mildred, she'll bounce back," Hud said. "How are you doing?"

"I'm okay. I'm just glad it's over."

Jackson could see the weight of all this on her. He wanted to scoop her and Natalie up and take them far away from this mess. But he knew the timing was all wrong. Allie had to deal with this before she would be free of Nick and his family.

"I did talk to the psychic Belinda took you to," Hud said. "She claims she didn't know what was planned. Mildred had given her a recording of Nick's voice that had been digitally altered with Drew helping with any extra words that were needed. She alleges she was as shocked as anyone when Nick said what he did."

"I believe her," Allie said.

"As for who shot your horse up in the mountains…" Hud rubbed a hand over his face. "I've arrested Drew for that. I can't hold him for long without evidence, but he does own a .22 caliber rifle and he did have access to the ranch."

"So that whole family gets off scot-free?" Jackson demanded.

Hud raised a brow. "I wouldn't say scot-free. I'd love to throw the book at Mildred and Drew, believe me. But neither will see jail time I'm afraid. Their justice will have to come when they meet their maker." Hud shook his head and turned to Jackson. "I heard Austin is recovering fine."

"It was touch and go for a while, but he's tough. The doctor said he will be released from the hospital in a week or so, but he is looking at weeks if not months before he can go back to work. He might actually get up to Montana to see the Texas Boys Barbecue joint before the grand opening."

"I suppose you're headed back to Texas then?" Hud asked. "Dana said Ford will be starting kindergarten his year?"

Jackson nodded. "I suppose I need to get a few things sorted out fairly soon."

ALLIE COULDN'T FACE the cabin. She had nothing but bad memories there. So she'd been so relieved when Dana had insisted she and Natalie stay in one of the cabins. All but one of them was now free since Laramie had gone back to Texas, and Hayes and McKenzie had bought a ranch down the highway with a large house that they were remodeling. Only Jackson and Ford were still in their cabin, not that

Ford spent much time there since he was having so much fun with his cousins.

The same with Natalie. Allie hardly saw her over the next few days. She'd gotten through the funerals of Sarah and a second one for Nick. Mildred had tried to make her feel guilty about Sarah's death. But when Mildred started insisting that Natalie come stay with her, Allie had finally had to explain to her mother-in-law that she wouldn't be seeing Nat and why.

Of course Mildred denied everything, insisting Sarah had been a liar and blamed everything on her poor mother.

"We're done," Allie said. "No matter what I decide to do in the future, you're not going to be a part of my life or Natalie's."

"I'll take you to court, I'll…" Mildred had burst into tears. "How can you be so cruel to me? It's because you have all my Nickie's money now. I can't hold my head up in this canyon anymore, my husband is divorcing me, Drew is selling out and leaving… Where am I supposed to go?"

"I don't care as long as I never have to see you." Allie had walked away from her and hadn't looked back.

"I don't want Nick's insurance money," she'd told Dana the day she and Natalie had moved into one of the ranch cabins.

"Use just what you need and put the rest away for Natalie. Who knows what a good education will cost by the time Nat goes to college? Then put that family behind you."

But it was her own family that Allie was struggling to put behind her, she thought as she saw Megan drive up in the ranch yard. Megan had been calling her almost every day. She hadn't wanted to talk to her. She didn't want to now, but she knew she had to deal with it, no matter how painful it was.

Stepping out on the porch, she watched her half sister get out of the car. Natalie, who'd been playing with the kids, saw her aunt and ran to her. Allie watched Megan hug Natalie to her and felt a lump form in her throat.

"We can talk out here," she told Megan as Natalie went to join her friends.

Allie took a seat on the porch swing. Megan remained standing. Allie saw that she'd been crying.

"I used to ask about you when I was little," Megan said. "I'd seen photographs of you and you were so pretty." She let out a chuckle. "I was so jealous of your green eyes and your dimples. I remember asking Dad why I got brown eyes and no holes in my cheeks."

Allie said nothing, just letting her talk, but her heart ached as she listened.

"I always wanted to be you," Megan said. "Dad wouldn't talk about your mother, so that made me all the more curious about what had happened to her. When I found out… I was half afraid when I met you, but then you were so sweet. And Natalie—" she waved a hand through the air, her face splitting into a huge smile "—I fell in love with her the moment I saw her. But I guess I was looking for cracks in your sanity even before Nick was killed and Mildred began telling me things. I'm sorry. Can you ever forgive me?"

Allie had thought that what she couldn't do was ever trust Megan again, especially with Natalie. But as she looked at her stepsister, she knew she had to for Natalie's sake. She rose from the chair and stepped to her sister to pull her into her arms.

They both began to cry, hugging each other tightly. There was something to this family thing, Allie thought. They might not be related by blood, but Allie couldn't cut Megan out of their lives, no matter where the future led them.

ALLIE WATCHED HER sister with Natalie and the kids. Megan, at twenty-three, was still a kid herself, she thought as she watched her playing tag with them. She knew she'd made the right decision and felt good about it.

She felt freer than she had in years. She'd also made up with Belinda. They would never be as close, not after her friend had kept her relationship with Nick from her. But they would remain friends and Allie was glad of it.

Belinda said she wanted her to meet the man in her life. Maybe Allie would, since it seemed that this time the relationship was serious.

Drew had tried to talk to her at the funeral, but she'd told him what she'd told his mother. She never wanted to see either of them again and with both of them leaving the canyon, she probably never would.

Beyond that, she didn't know. She would sell the cabin, Nick's pickup, everything she owned and start over. She just didn't know where yet, she thought as she saw Jackson coming up the mountainside.

He took off his Stetson as he approached the steps to her cabin and looked up at her. "Allie," he said. "I was hoping we could talk."

She motioned him up onto the porch. He looked so bashful. She smiled at the sight of his handsome face. The cowboy had saved her more times than she could count. He'd coming riding in on his white horse like something out of a fairytale and stolen her heart like an old-time outlaw.

"What did you want to talk about?" she asked. He seemed as tongue tied as Ford had been when he'd met Natalie.

"I…I…" He swallowed. "I love you."

Her eyes filled with tears. Those were the three little words she had ached to hear. Her heart pounded as she stepped to him. "I love you, Jackson."

He let out a whoop and picking her up, spun her around. As he set her down, he was still laughing. "Run away with me?"

"Anywhere."

"Texas?"

"If that's where you want to go."

"Well, here is the problem. You know my father, Harlan? I think he might just make a better grandfather than he ever did a father. I want Ford to have that."

She smiled. "Montana?"

"This is where I was born. I guess it is calling back my whole family. Did I tell you that my mother's new husband, Franklin, owns some land in the state? They're going to be spending half the year here. Hayes and McKenzie bought a place up the road and Tag and Lily will be living close by, as well. Dana said we can stay on the ranch until we find a place. The only thing we have to do is make sure our kids are in school next month."

"Montana it is then."

"Wait a minute." He looked shy again as he dropped to one knee. She noticed he had on new jeans and a nice Western dress shirt. Reaching into his pocket, he pulled out a ring box. "You're going to think I'm nuts. I bought this the day Tag and I went to pick up his rings for the wedding. I saw it and I thought, 'It's the same color as Allie's eyes.' Damned if I knew what I was going to do with it. Until now." He took a breath and let it out. "Would you marry me, Allie?"

She stared down at the beautiful emerald-green engagement ring set between two sparkling diamonds and felt her eyes widen. "It's the most beautiful thing I have ever seen."

He laughed. "No, honey, that would be you," he said as he put the ring on her finger, then drew her close and kissed her. "I can't wait to tell the kids. I have a feeling Ford and Natalie are going to like living in Montana on their very own ranch, with their very own horses and lots of family around them."

Allie felt like pinching herself. She'd been through so much, but in the end she'd gotten something she'd never dreamed of, a loving man she could depend on and love with all her heart. For so long, she'd been afraid to hope that dreams could come true.

She smiled as Jackson took her hand and they went to tell the kids the news.

* * * * *